Z.

I

Front

2023

II - Misguided Desires Series

Eminence Front is a work of fiction. Names, characters, places and incidents either are products of the author's imagination or are used fictitiously. Any resemblance to actual persons, living or deceased, events, or locales is entirely coincidental.

Edited by **Creech Enterprises**

Cover design by

Cover Photography by **Taleen Photography,** Blind Bay BC

https://taleenpileggiphotography.com/

Model- **Levi Eden**

Dedication

My biggest heartfelt thanks goes to my wonderful Editor, Jeanie at Creech Enterprises. Without her, I am nothing.

Next, I'd like to once again thank my friends and family for being so understanding with all the time with them I sacrificed in order to complete each novel I write. A big thank you is also necessary for each and every person who contributed to this edition, or inspired it. To my fantastic Photographer Taleen, you're so amazing, thank you for sharing my vision. Levi, my studly model, a big thank you to you as well for jumping in with such enthusiasm and vigor.

And last but not least, to my fellow sinful smuts; I hope you satiate yourself in the depths of this book and all it has to offer. Thank you for reading and for giving me a reason to write.

Table of Smut

The

PantyDropper Playlist

Into It- Chase Atlantic
Boss Bitch- Doja Cat
Falling- Alesso
Pretty Little Poison-Warren Zeiders
Thinkin' Bout Me- Morgan Wallen
Kiss It Better- Rihanna
Dancing With The Devil-Jelly Roll
Sin So Sweet-Warren Zeiders
Curiosity-Bryce Savage
I See Red- Everybody Loves an Outlaw

1
Coach

I strode down the terminal after disembarking the plane. It had been a decent flight for only my second time flying in my life. I had said goodbye to my home for the past twenty seven years just the previous morning. To say it had been emotional would have been an understatement. Wiping my mother's tears from her eyes following our final embrace before I walked through the doors onto the boarding bridge had been the hardest thing I had endured in my thirty-six years on this Earth. Aside from a few incidents from my childhood that I tried to bury deep down, of course.

My mother was always my constant. She understood me. She could read my silence and make sense of it, no words needed. Our eyes would meet and it was like having a full conversation. I knew I'd miss my home, the land, the sea, my siblings. But out of all those things, I knew I'd miss my mother the most.

I was not shy. I was just quiet. Thoughtful and observant, as my mother always described me.

My boots clicked against the white porcelain tile as I exited the bridge entering the airport and headed straight for the baggage claim. Wasting no time at all, I called a cab while I waited for my bags to emerge on the carousel.

I hadn't brought much, just the necessities. I'd fit it all into two large black suitcases and a carry-on. I reached for them one by one as they rotated around towards me and slung them onto a nearby trolley in order to steer them out to the awaiting cab in one trip.

I was determined to make a new life for myself. I had to make this trip, return to my roots. I can't explain why this was so important to me. It just always had been. Ever since I was nine years old and had witnessed the aftermath of my mother's injuries, inflicted by none other than my own father. I was repulsed . How a man could raise a hand to a woman, let alone a fist. It had scarred me, but probably for the better. I had molded my entire life since then to make amends for his actions. I did not want his poor judgment to reflect on me.

Once we relocated to Greece, we had made a home along the coastline in Nafpaktos, a gorgeous old village that captured the location's heritage. There I began my journey into the study of Brazilian jiu jitsu and martial arts.

For me, it had been a coping mechanism. As I was so quiet, I had no real vent for my feelings, and no one who could ever comprehend or understand. So I resorted to my own form of therapy. A way for me to work through my frustrations, and I worked hard. I'm sure I caused my mother more worry than she was willing to admit. She was supportive of my endeavors. I think she knew it was my way to cope. I had grown to really enjoy the art and entered multiple competitions. There were many victories and also failures, which I always viewed as opportunities for growth.

As I aged, I obtained my business degree. My long term goal was to open my own facility where I could teach others. Help others the way my own coach helped me. Now here I was, moving back to British Columbia, Canada to do just that.

My cabby opened the trunk as he saw me approach, and I lifted my bags in with ease. He clicked the trunk closed, and we both walked around to our prospective places, opened our doors and climbed in.

"Where to, Sir?"

"The nearest car rental establishment please."

"Rightio, there's a Budget car rental a few blocks from here."

"Perfect."

2

I parked the Budget rental car, a white Hyundai, in one of the assigned stalls. It didn't take more than five minutes to hand in the keys and I was out the door again. I had traveled five and a half hours from Vancouver to Salmon Arm, with no more than two stops. Gas, coffee and to void. I was ready to sleep.

My exhaustion finally setting in, I booked a room across the parking lot at the Super 8 motel. I was too tired to even eat. Between my flight and the drive, I was done. The clerk handed me the keys for room 109. Within seconds of entering the conservatively decorated room, I threw my bags down and collapsed on the bed, dead to the world.

When I finally woke, I squinted my eyes to the sun glaring through the window's only partially drawn drapes. I fumbled reaching for the alarm clock. It's red digital numbers read "10:04". *Dear Lord, I haven't slept in that long in over a decade.*

I stretched and rose up, still clothed. I made my way to the bathroom and splashed some water on my face, scrubbing the exertions of the past few days out of my pores. I gargled with a mouthful of the complimentary mouthwash left for me on the counter. Although my stomach was still empty, it felt good to have a fresh mouth again.

Eager for some food, I searched for a nearby restaurant. I got lucky, a Home restaurant was literally across the parking lot again on the far side of the Budget rental facility. I ordered a lumberjack's breakfast, and after a brief wait, I was finally able to chow down.

I guzzled two cups of hot black coffee and wolfed down every ounce of food on my plate. I looked up and found the charming young waitress smiling at me warmly as she offered to top me up again.

"No thank you." I held up my hand in protest.

She nodded

"Can I bring you your bill?"

"Yes please, that'd be great. I appreciate your service, Shelly."

At the mention of her name she flashed me an ear to ear smile and her cheeks flushed. She couldn't have been more than twenty-nine. She rushed away to grab my bill and promptly returned. I noticed she had drawn a smiley face on it for me, although I faintly made out the start of her phone number. She must have had second thoughts and changed it into a smiley face. Flattered, I left her some cash and a generous tip before striding out the door on my way to the nearest dealership. Two were in close proximity to my location. I just had to decide what brand I'd like to drive.

Three hours later, just before two in the afternoon, I drove out of the GM dealership with a second hand black Yukon SUV. While I waited for them to process my financial information, I had called the realtor I had been in contact with while still in Greece; Serena Walters. We had made arrangements to have a viewing that afternoon at quarter to three. Although it may seem spontaneous, I could assure anyone who asked, every move I made had been premeditated and meticulously thought out.

There was a reason I chose when I did to finally make my trip back to my hometown. I wasn't interested in being directly in town. In fact, I hated the idea of being here again. So when I was making all my plans, I purposefully looked in surrounding locations nearby to make my home. I had come across a gem.

Sorrento lay approximately twenty or so minutes from Salmon Arm. It was a nice short drive. My realtor was arranging her paperwork when I pulled up behind her. Her crimson red pencil skirt and suit jacket made her easy to spot.

"Pleasure to finally meet your acquaintance in person. You must be Mister..."

"Please, call me Coach. The pleasure's all mine, Serena." I interrupted her.

She extended her finely manicured hand to shake my own. I grasped it firmly and gave it a curt shake.

I could feel her eyes looking me up and down. I was no stranger to women eyeing me up. It was my gift as well as my curse. Who didn't love being adored? However, it made it hard to find something truly genuine. When people want to be with you just for being good looking, they never truly take the time to get to know the real you.

I shouldn't complain. I definitely didn't stop myself from enjoying the company of attractive women based on the fact that they only wanted me physically, when in fact I quite often only wanted them for their good looks as well. I wouldn't lie, I enjoyed the company of many. She bit her bottom lip subtly and glanced me over once more before she gestured me towards the property's driveway.

"Let me show you the place. I know you've traveled super far to finally lay your eyes on it."

"Yes, indeed."

I nodded my agreeance and held back a yawn, thinking once again of all the miles I traveled. On that note she spun around, and I followed her, trying not to watch her wiggling backside in that skin tight skirt. But I couldn't completely ignore it. I felt like a bull watching a matador's red silken cape swaying in the wind, taunting and teasing me.

"Here it is!"

Her arms spread wide, presenting the building to me as she swung the door to the shop open, knowing that it was the shop that had been my real interest. I lifted my eyes from mher captivating rear to first take in the facade and then the interior she was motioning me into.

"It needs a little work as I mentioned before, but it has a lot of potential."

I took it all in, I looked at the entire expanse of the building. The ceiling, walls, and floors. Opened cupboards to check the plumbing and located the water heater and electrical boxes. I would definitely be getting professionals to do a more thorough inspection, but as it stood, it passed my initial eye test.

Serena hit the nail on the head when she had said it needed work. The cement floors were chipped and the ceiling had a hole where a packrat had made it's dwelling. I needed to expand the whole building in order to accommodate my plans. The house on the other hand, which laid right next door, was very appropriate. A few renovations would be needed here and there. Otherwise it was more than suitable.

Serena must have noticed the look of approval on my face.

"Well? What do you think?" she inquired joyfully.

"I'd like to make an offer, all subject to the inspections of course, but it seems like it would work." Serena's eyes lit up, likely seeing dollar signs floating above my head.

"Fantastic! I'll start the paperwork first thing. What would you like to offer?"

"I'll try ten under what they're asking, see what they say."

The stakes were high with this bet. I didn't want to seem too eager and have the owners know they had the power, but I didn't want to aim too low either and have them completely dismiss me. I knew this was the place. I had to have it.

"Will do, Mr... uh, I mean Coach."

Her cheeks immediately flushed as she corrected herself.

"Is there anything else I can show you?"

Her eyes floated down and lingered on my crotch a second too long before looking up at me again through her long mascaraed lashes. I could only take so many hints without making a move. After all, I was still a man.

3

Serena dawned her heels again and began ambling towards the door, adjusting her pencil skirt as she went. It was still askew when she reached the doorway and began tucking her shirt back in and sweeping her artificially blonde hair out of her face. I didn't dare tell her it would take a hell of a lot more "fixing" to resurrect her ensemble back to its prior professional state.

"It was a pleasure meeting you, Coach." She winked at me.

"I'll put in that offer right away for you."

I chuckled.

"Well I'm just going to pretend it's mine already, seeing how I've already christened it."

She gave me a goofy grin and laughed.

"You caught me at a weak moment." She shrugged her shoulders.

"No regrets. Lock up when you leave."

She gave a little wave and then hurried out the door, her step a little lighter than it was just a half hour ago.

I took one last fleeting glance at the presently abandoned shop before closing the door and locking the deadbolt. I had big dreams for this place.

I returned to my hotel room to patiently await the news that would either make me or break me. Knowing full well it'd be the longest wait of my life, and not to mention would likely take a few weeks. It was best for me to start making other arrangements and focus on other details to help kill the time. So that's what I did.

I had uniforms designed, measured and ordered. Located high quality mats. Sourced out some affordable quality lumber, nails, supplies and laborers to assist me if the deal went through. I started filling out the applications for building licenses and permits within the bylaws.

I knew I was being presumptuous, but either way, I knew if I found any other location I'd have to do the same things. So might as well get a head start on it.

I was lucky that I chose to bank with a mainstream bank. It made the transition from Greece to here much easier and my funds readily available without further delays.

It was a long two weeks, but Serena finally called me on a Friday.

"Congratulations! You're now a home owner!"

"That's awesome! Thank you! I was starting to get worried."

"These things take time unfortunately. Being as the owners had basically abandoned the property, there were a few more hoops we had to jump through. But we did it! You can collect the keys tomorrow at the office. I'll have Trudy leave them at the front for you, as I won't be there tomorrow, being the weekend and all. Make sure you go get home insurance right away as well!"

"Check, check and check!" I smiled through the phone.

"I appreciate your hard work, Serena, thank you."

"You're most welcome Coach, just doing my job though. Maybe I'll see you around sometime. I hope I will anyway. Until then, best of luck to you."

"You as well. Bye." And with that the call ended, and a new chapter of my life began.

4

I pulled into my driveway. Felt good to say that. *My driveway.* I wasn't about to spend any more money staying in that motel for another night. Not when I had my own place. I had purchased a bed frame cheap online and found a few essentials at the local thrift shop, Churches. I had lucked out finding a mattress sale at Garage furniture. I wasn't about to try my luck with a second hand one. Groceries were another item I had taken the liberty of grabbing on my way out of town after picking up the keys from Trudy. I was fully loaded and ready to spend my first night in my own home.

I took a moment to sit and stare out my windshield and take in the view, reveling in the moment. It had finally happened. I had made it.

The lock on my door unlatched as I pulled the handle to swing it open. Stepping out onto the yellowing grass, I sucked in a deep breath of that crisp fall air and made my way, with arms full of moving boxes stacked one atop another, to the entranceway of *my* house. I unlocked the door, set down the boxes, turned and strode out to the shop. I pushed open the old wooden door and walked in looking all around once more. There was a lot of work that had to be done. Renovations were set to start up the following day. Myself, I'd be starting up in the morning getting a headstart on it all, eager to make my dreams a reality.

5

At the crack of dawn, I could hear a neighbor's rooster welcoming the rising sun with his shriek *cock-a-doodle doo*!

That was my signal. With a mighty stretch, I yawned and rose for the day. I had taken the liberty of setting up the bed as well as all the other items I had purchased, and put away the basic necessities like dishware and towels the night before. I wanted to wake with a sense of belonging. It had worked. I felt revitalized, at home and at peace, ready to take on the challenges at hand.

I always started my days with a morning workout- push-ups, sit-ups, jump rope. I didn't have my punching bag with me, so I strapped a throw cushion to a tree outside. It worked effectively enough. My blood was pumping, and a quick shower charged me up even more.

Stepping out of the shower, I grabbed one of the new towels from the hook I had slung it on and wrapped it around my waistline. The mirror was right across from me, and my shower had been so quick the fog hadn't blurred out my image yet. I stood taking in my appearance. I stood at about 6' 3". My tan skin was both hereditary as well as enhanced from all my years in Nafpaktos. My muscles etched deeply into my skin. No one ever had to take a second glance at me to know it wasn't a good idea to mess with me. For this I was proud. All my hard work in the gym and performing jiu-jitsu paid off.

I grabbed my brush and ran it through my chestnut hair, cut short with a bit of length on top that I could still style it. My gray eyes, my mother always told me came from my father, thus making me hate them. However, she always told me they were soft, observant and warm, which my father's were not.

I placed down the brush, grabbed my electric shaver and trimmed my facial hair. It had grown exponentially in the past days in preparation of my move-in. I liked to leave scruff, as a full beard seemed like more of a target for grappling hands to pull during a fight, and I didnt want to be completely bare. I felt the scruff at least showed my age, which helped kids to know to show me respect in the gym. With a *click,* I turned off the shaver and placed it back on the bathroom vanity, trading it in for my toothbrush. I took great care of my teeth. I believed they gave a person's first impression, and I enjoyed giving a good first impression.

With all my morning tasks complete, I decided to skip breakfast and go straight to work. I had an excavator and dump truck coming at noon that day and wanted to get a head start before they arrived.

All morning I had worked, marking off the demo areas, measuring and flagging for rebuild, shutting off and removing the present plumbing. Found the beam I would start the addition from and took my chainsaw to cut along it so removal of the demolished portion would come away easily without damage to the existing portion I wanted left intact. That was hard work. I had turned the power off as well, as a safety precaution, and had called Fortis regarding the location of my gas lines. I didn't need to be hitting one of those whilst digging the addition's foundation, that's for sure.

Noon rolled around quicker than I could have ever anticipated. Thank goodness I had started early. A hefty bearded fellow named Don collaborated with me. I told him my plans and showed him the flagged areas. He explained his process prior to beginning after a firm handshake.

Demolition was fast work. I watched as the excavator ripped off the front half of the shop I had sawed apart and then scooped the rubble into the awaiting dump truck's bucket. Within the hour, there was nothing left of the tattered portion of the shop, and Don efficiently began digging the foundation.

As there was nothing for me to do while they worked, I grabbed some lunch and a cold beer to enjoy, then settled down to make some phone calls.

6

.ll when construction on my shop was finally finished. s and I had worked diligently every day, weekends try to get it done before the snow.

.l in a small cluster of red and yellow late autumn leaves that ,inning to brown, looking up at my masterpiece. Taking it all v fully functional and ready for business.

had come up with the name The Brazilian Jiu Jitsu Wild Dogs D, or as I preferred it abbreviated; BJJ-WD Club. Wild Dogs was e unofficial mascot/team name for when my students would be :ntered into competitions. I had a fierce coyote baring and gnashing his teeth designed for the logo. A big sign hung along the front of the building with a spotlight directed on it. You couldn't miss it.

I couldn't even begin to describe the pride I was feeling for the amount of accomplishment achieved in such a short amount of time.

I walked inside the big shop door to also take in the interior of the gym. Large black mats covered the floor in the fighting and grappling ring area. The walls also had thick blue and gray mats secured up their sides. The cement floor at the gym's entrance had some rubber mats and an area for footwear and jackets to be hung.

A desk greeted the front door, and the logo was painted on the wall behind it as well as a giant mural of the logo along the back wall behind the grapple zone. The rest of the walls were painted a creamy white and were draped with a variety of sizes of *gis,* the traditional uniform used in the art of jiu jitsu. This way I could accommodate my future students with an outfit instead of having to order and wait for the gis to arrive. Students could then get started the same day they arrive.

Various pads for boxing and kickboxing also lined one wall, beneath the gis, ready for use. Above the ring was a spectator area which was built with the new construction, as well as a hidden change area beneath the spectators view pad. I had another hidden room down there as well. I hadn't decided what to do with it exactly, so left it a blank slate for when I finally figured it out.

A bathroom lay in the back corner of the gym, unisex and included a shower as well, an idea I really liked. I knew exactly how much one could perspire during a class.

A big digital clock was positioned adjacent to the match zone. I could control it with my phone in order to time drills, and set grapple times. A detail I thought would be super convenient if I were to host tournaments at my facility as well.

A series of fluorescent pot lights lit the entire gym, creating a sheen from the mats and the fresh paint that reflected the light back.

I puffed my chest in admiration, and a diminutive smile crossed my lips. I was set to open my doors to business the very next day. The website had gone live days before, and I had already started receiving phone calls inquiring about classes. I had been prepared to be underwhelmed at the beginning until word of mouth got out and more business drummed up; however, I was starting to think maybe it wouldn't be so slow after all.

7

Three o'clock in the afternoon finally rolled around. I had been subconsciously watching the clock for hours. I was more than ready, but had tried to find many light handed tasks to keep me preoccupied until the start of my very first class.

I realized I was holding my breath and allowed myself to release the pent up CO2 with a *whoosh*. As I did, the door flung open. Several families all rushed in, storming the entrance way of the gym with water bottles and bags in tow. I greeted them all, introduced myself, and then began assigning gis to all the participants.

It took longer than I anticipated to gear everyone up, because even more kids than I had expected showed up. I guess word of mouth traveled faster than I anticipated. Each parent told another parent friend about their kid or kids signing up for jiu jitsu, and then the friend decided to bring their kids as well, and so on and so forth.

I felt a smile curling up on my lips. This was great, exactly what I had hoped for; actually, it exceeded what I'd hoped for.

The amount of kids ages five to twelve damn near filled a huge portion of the gym. I instructed them to all line up against one wall, from oldest to youngest, and directed the parents to the viewing area. I noted that even the viewing area wasn't going to hold all the parents that had accompanied their children. I thought fast and walked over, pushing a few of my kick pads out of the way, clearing an area. I waved my hand and guided the remaining adults over.

"Here folks, feel free to find spots on the mats to sit and watch."

They looked uncertain, but at my open armed gesture they filtered over, locating spots to sit or lean and observe.

The kids were all talking excitedly amongst themselves. A hush fell over the room as I approached the center of the mats. Everyone's eyes were plastered on me, adults and children alike.

"Greetings all! Welcome to the Brazilian Jiu Jitsu Wild Dogs Club. Thank you for your interest in learning martial arts. I can assure you, it is both a fun and rewarding venture. For some of you, that's all it is, just *fun*. But for some of you, it could be more. It could be self-defense. It could be self-esteem building, and for a few, it may even be a competitive or career building move. All these reasons for joining jiu jitsu, are the *right* reasons to join. There is no wrong reason to want to try."

I peered around the room, eyeing them all up, letting the weight of my words sink in.

"My only requests from you all while you're here are that you always listen, and always respect. Jiu jitsu can be very dangerous if not done correctly, or if you don't listen to your sparring partner and stop. So I need you all to always pay attention. If your partner taps out, you let go immediately. No questions asked, you just stop and release them. Does everybody understand?"

A synchronized, "Yes coach," echoed around the gym.

"Good! Ok, now everyone circle up and let me go over a few basic moves before we do a warm up and start."

With that, feet started shuffling this way and that, and they managed to align themselves in a somewhat circular fashion surrounding me.

Eyes and ears were attentive, and within minutes I was wrapping up the verbal lesson for that class and moving on to some warm up exercises, prior to letting them practice. I could feel the parents eyes watching and listening as well, absorbing what I was teaching and being ready to reiterate to their young ones later on.

The rush of energy throughout the warm up was astounding. I'd never really experienced a class from a teacher's standpoint before. I made the decision then to do the warm ups right away from then on. Kids had all been in school most of the day, and had energy to burn. They needed the opportunity to burn off some steam prior to learning more. Getting to release some of that energy might help them absorb the lessons better as well as listen.

I used a volunteer from the group to demonstrate the few basic first moves I had planned on coaching them through that day before pairing them up to spar.

The combustion of excited little voices and bustle of feet across the mats was music to my ears as they all set forth partnered up to attempt the execution of the moves they had just learnt. The sound of grunting and laughter consumed the air.

I made my way around the area, side stepping bodies wrestling on the floor, correcting their positioning and technique as I went. The adults observed and socialized. I saw many catch themselves as they would go to cheer their kids on, and reel their shouts of encouragement back in.

In the code of conduct agreement on my website, it explained that my gym was not the setting to cheer for one individual over another. That here, parents just watched and supported with their presence. I wanted a very inclusive and non-judgemental atmosphere. I was glad to see the parents had read and accepted the context I had laid out in the contract. It really contributed to the children's learning environment and also how they grew as people. I wanted humble students, not inflated egos. That mindset always led to trouble.

The hour flew by. By classes end, the air was hot and muggy with the twenty six or so sweaty kids' bodies that were walking off the mats content and tired.

"Thank you, Coach!"

The appreciative verse echoed out of every little mouth as they exited the gym. I high-fived their hands as they walked past me, letting each one know what a great job they'd done.

I had a fifteen minute break between that class and the next, but already the thirteen to seventeen year olds were filing in with ear to ear grins adorning their faces.

Learning from my prior mistakes, after getting everyone's gis on, I commenced the warm up before leading into the lesson then grappling. It worked really well. Thus my routine was built.

By night's end, I knew I would continue to have steadily full classes. The number of participants had far exceeded my expectations for my first session, and I couldn't wait to do it all again.

8

As the months passed by, word continued to spread about my gym, and my class size reached a point I had to make the decision to expand.

I purchased another building in the city of Kamloops which was an hour past Sorrento and an hour and a half past Salmon Arm.

It was a big commitment, both in regards to investment as well as mileage, but I had no choice. My business was growing faster than I could keep up, and my gym in Sorrento was overflowing its max capacity. Bylaws and insurance would have my head if they found out, and that was too great a risk for me to take.

As it turned out, the majority of my new clientele were traveling to my present location from Kamloops, Lee Creek, and Celista areas. So opening a gym in a bigger center like Kamloops made a lot of sense. I knew the bills would all get paid. It was the commitment of splitting my time between the two gyms that concerned me.

I had asked a Kamloops local realtor by the name of Josh Davis to assist me in my hunt for the right building to accommodate my plans. It only took a few weeks, and we went through a series of options he had procured. Some spoke to me, but there was always at least one thing that wasn't ideal. Josh kept digging for me. I think he was just as eager as I was to find the right place.

Turned out he was quite the athlete himself and was interested in taking some martial arts classes. He had begun putting the bug in my ear to open up for adult classes as well.

I had never thought to teach adults before, I'm not sure why. I had always cut it off at teens. He made some good points though, and it could draw in more income to cover the costs of another gym faster.

It would mean longer nights at both gyms though, plus the travel time to the Kamloops gym. I already knew I'd be having to spend more days of the week at the bigger center in order to make any kind of profit. Being in a higher populated area would mean increasing the numbers of students. That would equate to more classes as well.

That meant I'd be stretching myself thin for a few years until the buildings were paid off, but once that was done, I'd be doing quite well and would potentially be set for life.

The idea of adding adult classes did make a lot of sense. I kept rolling it around in my mind, mulling it over and over. How could I turn down the chance to really make my business take off even more?

So with that in mind, I concluded I'd be adding adult classes in both locations once the bigger gym was purchased and up and running.

Josh didn't disappoint. In six weeks time, he found me the perfect place. Right in the heart of the city too, but on a quiet street in the industrial park, right near the college and the Canada Games Aquatic Center. The price was right, and it wouldn't take much in renovations to create exactly what I envisioned for the space.

I signed the mortgage papers on a Monday, and by Thursday the following week, the place was officially mine. This time I hired a crew to assist me with the renovations and design. What a relief that was! A few extra sets of hands made light work.

Josh assured me he'd be one of my first adult students, and had a list of friends who were also interested in attending. All in all, I got a new friend out of this business transaction, an additional income source, and an invested interest. Just another thing I was thankful for.

The new gym opened in May. A weird month to start, but as I'd only begun the process of purchase shortly into the new year, May seemed as good a time as any. I was offering classes year round, no summers off like most gyms. I wanted people to have access anytime they desired, and there weren't too many places I'd rather be than in my gyms. It was truly my passion.

Although at the end of the day, once all classes had ended, I'd retire to my house at night. I couldn't help but feel the gnawing loneliness starting to creep up on me. I still spoke with my mother often, but what I desired was companionship.

Lustful affairs and one night stands weren't cutting it anymore. Perhaps I had arrived at that age where I was looking to settle down. I wasn't sure. All I knew was that there was an emptiness that I couldn't resolve. But my nightly promiscuity at least held it at bay, and so I kept on.

Ever since the Sorrento gym had opened up, I'd enjoyed my fair share of company from the single moms of my students. A bit *faux pas* on the professional end of things, but in small towns, there weren't many options that didn't cross one line or another.

I did my best to avoid the mothers I knew were in fact married. I couldn't believe how many there were that still seemed to be seeking my attention despite their marital status. But infidelity was something I really tried to steer away from. That would be bad for business. However, I was always up for a good time...

I had finally found a purpose for the bare room next to the changeroom in my Sorrento gym after one fateful event before a class. She was the mother of one of the kids in my teens group.

Connie Parker. I could constantly feel her hazel eyes boring into my back during class. She'd scan me up and down hungrily during any conversation we had together, whether pertaining to the weather, her bill payments, or her son's progress in class.

Her ombre dirty blonde hair hung around her face, framing it. Mascaraed lashes always donned her pale face and gave her that doe-eyed look. Her thin frame always sported clothes fit for a girl, not a woman. Crop tops, tight low rise jeans, A-cup bralettes that could be seen either through her shirt or rips in them. I had the feeling she struggled in providing, did her best, but was also torn with her desire to find love and also to still be young herself.

She must have had her son at a young age. I assumed around fourteen. Her son was fifteen, and I didn't think Connie could be any older than thirty. She was trying, and I admired her for her efforts in raising her boy by herself and still trying to offer him extras, like jiu jitsu.

He was a good student, eager and driven. You could see the hardness in his eyes as he landed every punch and arm barred sparring partners. He had a hardness that doesn't come with a pampered life.

I'd like to say it started with dinner out, or even exchanging phone numbers, but I'd be lying.

The age five to twelve class had just ended and were barreling out the doors. My fifteen minute break was about to start. I turned up the music in order to build up momentum for the next class.

I had received word that afternoon that my older sister was expecting her second child, and I was to be an uncle again. I was happy for her, and congratulated her and her husband. But it triggered that emptiness again, that incessant want.

That's when Connie and her boy walked in early for class. Cooper, her son, greeted me and then went to change. His routine was to always do his own thorough warm up before class. Connie approached me as always to say hello. Her doe eyes were even wider than normal. Her soft faltering voice always so subdued.

Her submissiveness annoyed me. I wanted her to grow some backbone, and speak firmly. Show some real confidence, not the fake guise she presented with her underaged clothing and makeup. Alas, she was not one of my students, and my reach only went so far.

"Hey, Coach, how are you today?" She practically squeaked.

"Good, Connie, how about yourself?"

"Alright I guess, umm, I started a new job and I know it's a big ask, but I was wondering if I could start dropping Cooper off at three when the younger class is on? He could help out, assist you with teaching or tidy up in exchange?"

I could hear the desperation in her voice. Her voice wavered with each word she spoke.

"I don't see that being a problem, Connie. He's a good kid and would be a great contribution to my younger class. A second pair of eyes and hands is always an asset."

I could see the relief wash over her, and a smile flashed across her lips.

"Ohhh, thank you so much! I wasn't sure what I was going to do. I really need this job. Thank you! Maybe I can bring dinner sometime to show my appreciation."

I eyed hers and Cooper's thin frames, knowing it wasn't just genetics at play there.

"No, that's not necessary. It'll be great to have his assistance, and that's thank you enough."

I didn't want to embarrass her, nor take away from their dinner table. I wanted her to feel like instead she was doing me a favor. I could see her eyes glossing up, and her chest swell, the smile remained. A look arose on her face, and her stance changed. What was this? I'd swear it was a wave of...courage?

"Perhaps, you'd let me thank you in some other way then?"

She didn't hide her eyes as she surveyed my body slowly this time. Not her usual scared flitting eyes. Her gaze then locked mine. *Was she...propositioning me?*

She must have read my expression, and her smile widened. She glanced around. No one else had arrived for class yet, and Cooper was preoccupied with his punching bag drills.

Turning back to me, she lifted her arms and placed her hands on my chest. She began pushing me backwards into the empty open door beneath the gym's stairs.

"Connie, you don't have to do anything like this. I'm more than happy to help out, and it'd be my pleasure to have Cooper assist me."

I was walking backwards with her, but I wanted to make absolutely certain this wasn't about to be some sort of payment plan.

"No, I want to...I've wanted to for a long while. I just never had the opening."

Not allowing her gaze to leave mine, she reached behind her back and shut the door behind her. Bathed in darkness with only a small slit of light cast beneath the door, she boldly made her move.

Pushing her body against me she tiptoed up and pulled my head down to kiss me. Her lips tasted like cherry chapstick, and her skin smelt faintly of cigarettes and rising dough. I broke free of her kiss long enough to utter.

"I have a class in less than thirteen minutes."

She let out a giggle, purely amused.

"I only need three minutes."

My growing erection sprung at those words, going rock hard instantly. Where on earth was this new found confidence of hers coming from? It was freaking sexy!

8.5

Connie

I finally had him! For months I'd watched this man from a shy distance, approaching only when I absolutely had to. I had no idea what piqued my courage this afternoon. I guess I had mulled over so many propositions in my mind throughout the months my son had been attending jiu jitsu, it was almost a practice makes perfect scenario.

His kindness over letting me drop Cooper off early so I could try to maintain this new job, I had to repay him in some way. I couldn't physically pay him extra money, things were so tight already financially.

I'd be lying if I said it was *just* because I wanted to "repay" his kindness. It was more than that. He was so fucking fine. I knew all the other moms there saw it too, and I could hear all their whispers while I watched.

I always distanced myself slightly away from the others. I didn't like the hen house effect. I was quiet, and not much into gossip. Mostly because I'd always been the topic of the gossip for so many years. I'd rather not partake in something I loathed so much, but I did hear them talk about him. Just because I chose not to partake, didn't mean I didn't agree with their words.

"I'd love to wrestle him down!"

"My husband wonders why I'm so passionate about our kids' jiu jitsu. HE is the reason!"

"Thank goodness your husband doesn't attend, or he'd totally know it wasn't because you're watching your kids."

"Well, I think one look around the room at all our gawking faces would tell him, none of us are really here to watch our kids."

"Well, I like watching, but I'd be lying if I said my focus didn't go astray."

They went on and on. I agreed though. I loved watching Cooper, but there was something about that man that I had a hard time peeling my eyes off of him in order to watch my son. Being a mom, that was a hard thing to admit.

I spent hours each week admiring and fantasizing. Taking in his tan skin and tall muscular build. His tousled, short cropped, chestnut hair. He had the most intense gray eyes that bore into you. I swear he could see into my soul, see my desire, and that was super intimidating.

I was even more nervous around him than I was around most people. He made me feel raw and vulnerable, looking through all my layers and seeing what lay beneath.

I knew this was likely just a weird thing I had concocted in my mind. Imagine, thinking some random human could peer into my soul with one look. But alas, he reduced me to a quivering pile of bones every time I saw him.

What I wouldn't give to be with a man like that even for just one night. Someone strong and passionate. Someone who had their shit together. Someone so sexy he wouldn't even have to say the right thing to cause my loins to become wet with want.

Now, here I was. I was in this moment and I had the opportunity. I couldn't let it slip through my fingers. He wasn't refusing, or turning me down. He was only somewhat resistant due to being on the brink of his next class starting. That I could understand. But I assured him, I didn't need long.

It had been forever, it seemed, since I had been with a real man. One that could do the job right and one that actually wanted to service as well. And he was definitely the man I wanted to service!

Pressing him into that darkened room under the stairs, I had been eyeing this location for weeks now. It was so hidden in the shadows, no one ever really acknowledged it. It was like a long forgotten space, nobody paid it any mind. No one but me anyhow.

The amount of fantasies I had drummed up that involved this little room and Coach could last me a lifetime.

For these few minutes, he was mine, all mine. I pulled at his tee, hiking it up his abdomen. His height had me at a loss though, as I was far too short to get it over his head. However he kindly obliged me and pulled it the rest of the way off. I took advantage of the free seconds and yanked mine off as well, throwing that and my hoodie on the ground, wanting to feel his warm flesh pressed against my own.

I'd done myself a solid that morning by not wearing a bra, one less thing to tackle now.

I felt his body, caressing each ripple of every pronounced muscle. I leaned up as high as I could, kissing him. He leaned down meeting my lips. His tongue soft and soothing. He didn't maul my face like most guys, shoving their tongues so far down my throat I'd gag. No, this was sensual, and passionate.

I had no time to waste. I continued kissing him whilst untying his gi pants. I could feel his massive erection pushing against my abdomen. He was as eager as I was, and that was such a turn on.

Finally getting through that knot, his pants fell at his feet. The light under the door casting its pale glow just barely illuminated his body for me to feast my eyes. I'd always imagined what he would look like under his clothes. But the fantasies didn't even come close to the reality.

Every muscle was defined and prominent. He looked as if he was chiseled by a proficiently talented artist. A trimmed patch of chest hair added some softness to his hard etched look, and a small treasure trail guided me down. His girthy manhood loomed, hovering in mid air. It's thickness surpassed only by its length.

Without hesitating, I immediately plunged down on him. My mouth was watering for it! I could hear him gasp as my mouth first made contact, and he hissed in pleasure as I sucked his full length, choking only slightly as I had to stuff it down my throat in order to accommodate it all. His well groomed pubes held in his delectable scent.

I tried hard to think of what scent it even was, a mix of pheromones, leather and perhaps fabric softener? Whatever it may be, I breathed it in sufficiently with each plunge down. To me it was heavenly!

His fingers entangled into my hair using it as reigns, stroking it, letting me know I was doing a good job.

I slathered his cock in saliva, lubricating it for my lips to slide down his shaft with no resistance. Again and again. I squeezed his ass and played with his balls. Massaging them as I worked, wanting to leave no place unnoticed.

Through the door I could faintly hear footsteps above the music as more families began to arrive, and knew I didn't have long. I sucked him as far as I could down and then picked up the pace, letting his orgasm build with the momentum. However, he had other plans.

Grabbing my upper arms he pulled me to standing and frantically unbuttoned my jeans. He tugged at them a little then paused momentarily. I think waiting for my approval, to which I nodded and kissed him again as he yanked them all the way down and I kicked them off. They'd no sooner hit the floor that he then scooped me up.

His hands grasped my ass cheeks, splaying them out as he wrapped my legs around him. I held onto his neck for dear life.

His dick needed no guidance, it was so stiff, he was able to drag it down my eager slit and with no resistance at all as he pushed up inside me. I was saturated with the excitement of it all, and feeling his swollen hog glide into me had me instantly clamping my teeth on his shoulder to stifle my moans.

He thrust in again and again, bouncing me up and down on his meaty cock. His dick slamming into my g-spot effortlessly. I clawed his back with my left hand while my right remained holding onto his neck. It was all I could do. I found myself panting in his ear, sucking on his ear lobe, and tasting his sweat. Savoring it!

I could feel my juices pouring down his shaft onto his balls with each and every plunge in. My pussy grasped his dick tightly every time he hit that sought after spot. He had its location memorized now, and his thrusts were coming in faster succession, pounding into me.

His grip tightened on my ass, and he humped profoundly deeper. I could feel a knot at the base of his dick swelling and slowly rising up his shaft.

It was all so lustful and fast, I wished we could prolong it. But I knew before we had even started, this was the only way it could happen; fleetingly.

My bare chest pressed into his and I listened to him breathing, panting hard now, feeling his muscles jerk with the effort. His sheer strength showed as he pummeled my pussy whilst heaving me up and down in the air as silently as possible.

My clit was rubbing against his body with each quick paced thrust, the steady flow of moisture saturating her and allowing me even more satisfaction. Our bodies were now audibly smacking against one another, and I reckoned we were both grateful for the music drowning us out.

It was now or never. I lifted my legs up, pointing my toes at the ceiling. This gave him a whole new angle to slam, and god what an angle! We both succumbed to the pleasure this added depth gave us. My toes began to curl, and my clit hummed with my hovering orgasm. I was trying to hold out, waiting for him.

I didn't have to wait long. Within seconds, I felt that ever rising knot swell, and in the nick of time he pulled out. I bit his shoulder once more to muffle my shrieks of ecstasy. Hot cum was shooting all over my ass, and he clung to me as his body jerked a few more times as he finished his release.

I didn't want to let go of him. We both lingered for a moment, coming back to reality. He had a class of students waiting for him, and here I was, covered in his jizz. He lowered me back down to the ground, and I snatched my shirt up, using it to wipe his gooey lukewarm puddles off my body.

I clothed in my hoodie and tugged my panties and jeans back on, shoving my damp shirt in the kangaroo pouch of the hoodie. Coach was dressed again already too.

"I'll walk out and you can follow in a few minutes." He instructed. His coachly tone had returned. The moment over; he was back to business as usual. I nodded my agreeance, and he slipped out stealthily. I don't think anyone even noticed him until he B-lined for the center of the mats to greet his students.

I continued to wait. I wasn't ready to leave. I was still in disbelief that it actually happened. Had the damp t-shirt not been a reminder, nor the after orgasm tingle that remained buzzing in my crotch, I probably wouldn't have believed it had.

A few more moments passed before I creaked the door open just enough to sneak out. I was back to my usual mousey self and went seemingly unnoticed as I slunk over to my usual spot and sat to watch.

Little did I know, but somebody indeed had noticed.

9

Coach

Rebecca Carlyle, one of the most outspoken moms in both my gyms. She lived in Celista and would drive between both locations to cater to her kids, Kyle and Sophie. Kyle was twelve and Sophie was nine.

Becky, I could only estimate to be in her late forties. She was a stay at home mom. Prior to having kids, she had worked in an insurance broker's office and was known for her sharp tongue and opinionated views, or so I'd heard.

I hate to presume, but I had a feeling that was perhaps one of the reasons she hadn't returned to her broker position once her kids were of school age.

I had no idea what her ex-husband did, but I gathered he worked away and made a decent dollar.

Becky had a reputation, to say the least. She always knew everyone's business. In fact, she made it her business to know.

I tried to steer clear, knowing full well her fancy for me. *I know how vain that sounds, and I'm honestly not trying to be. But you can usually tell when someone's attracted to you, especially when that someone was so outspoken about it.*

Whenever I walked by her, I couldn't help but feel like I was a midnight snack. She'd let out a hoot or a holler, untie her signature kerchief she always wore and fan herself. Whistle. Make comments about my "hiney." I had to bite my tongue and walk away. It made me really able to empathize with women at nightclubs.

So when Becky approached me that day and made the physical effort to block me from veering out of her way, I knew I was in for trouble.

"I happened to notice your little, uh, business transaction there, Coach." She said in that matter of fact, nasally tone of hers.

"Business transaction? I have no idea what you're talking about."

I finally managed to step around her and busied myself straightening my new stock that had just been delivered.

"Oh, sure ya do." She smiled maliciously, chewing her gum in her lip smacking manner.

"No, I really don't. Please enlighten me."

I didn't want to give her the time of day. I knew people like Becky. They only wanted to talk to you if they wanted something from you or had something on you. I cringed to know what her angle was.

"With little Miss Parker," her eyebrow raised.

My heart stopped. *Fuck.*

I feigned ignorance.

"I still have no idea what you mean, Ms. Carlyle."

"Oh, I'm quite sure you do. I saw with my very own eyes you both leaving that dusty old cubby under the stairs the other day. I can't imagine what sort of discussions you might require to be had in a dark closet?"

Double fuck.

I stopped unpacking and turned to face her.

"I'm just doing her a favor, she started a new job and needed to be able to drop Cooper off early, that's it."

Her eyes narrowed and the twisted smile of hers crept onto her face again.

"Yes, that was quite the favor. How very... selfless of you." She nodded.

I could tell she didn't buy it.

"Listen, I don't want details. You keep it to yourselves. But keep in mind, I do know. And since you're so generous with favors and all...I could really use a helping hand."

She eyed me and gave an open mouthed wink, her wad of gum completely visible on her snakelike tongue. I sighed.

I didn't want the wrong kind of public attention around town, and if there were going to be any negative reviews, it would most definitely be from THIS woman.

"What do you want?"

"Now that's more like it!" Her big yellowed toothy grin flashed at me, and I shuddered. I had a bad feeling about this.

"I want what she got." She was circling me now.

I felt once again like a piece of meat for sale at a market.

"And what exactly do you think she *got* Ms. Carlyle? Do you want your kids to work for me while you hold down a new job?"

"I'm not an idiot, Coach. I'm going to be point blank. I want a quality ride. A hot young stud like you, I want the full deal. Down and dirty."

I felt myself wince. The utter thought of any action matching those words with that woman was cringeworthy.

Noting my hesitation, all friendliness left her voice.

"Or else..."

She left the end up to my interpretation, but I knew exactly what she was hinting at. She'd ruin both mine and Connie's reputations. What she'd spread around would be far more twisted than anything I could even make up. I couldn't believe I had gotten myself into this mess. I gave in on a weak moment. These were the consequences. I had to compromise though, otherwise she'd entrap me forever.

"Once! That's all you'll get. If you try anything funny or go back on your word, I'll try you for slander, understand?"

She mulled it over, squinting her crows feet at me. I could tell she was weighing her options. I knew she had wanted an ongoing affair, but that I was NOT willing to do. Once was going to be hellish enough.

"Deal. But you can't refuse any of my requests."

I cringed again.

"Ok, fine. Deal."

And with that I sold my soul for her silence.

9.5
Becky

It was time to collect. I picked up my cell and dialed.

"Hello?"

"It's time, lover. I'll send you a pin. You'd better be here pronto."

With that, I hung up. I knew he'd show; he'd be a fool not to.

Twenty minutes later I heard my phone ring.

"Where are you? I'm here, I don't see you."

"I'm 'round back having a smoke. See you in a sec."

I went back to inhaling another long drag. He'd come find me.

It was only about three minutes later, he strode up to me looking less than enthralled. He wore some dark relaxed slim fit jeans and a black Lamb of God t-shirt. He looked good for his choice of casual attire.

"Where are we exactly?" He looked around, unsure what to make of our location.

"It's a friend's pad, but he's basically turned it into a nightclub. Not much of a night life here in the Shuswap, have to do what you can."

I butted out my cigarette on the cracked cobblestone patio and hooked my finger through his belt loop.

"Let's go."

I led him through the crowd, seeking out something to inebriate him a bit prior to our arrangement. It wasn't fun if only one of us was cutting loose.

A keg lay off to the side of what was once the kitchen, now with its cupboard doors off and graffitied black sharpie marker labeling it *Bar*. I requested two red dixie cups for the keg. However, the "bartender" looked to be tripping and was staring off at a bug zapper sitting atop the fridge.

I shrugged and pushed myself through the duct taped cardboard swinging saloon door and grabbed them myself.

Pouring our cups full, Coach watched, looking really uncertain and squeamish about the whole setting. For a young fella, he sure didn't know how to loosen up and enjoy.

I forced the beer into his hands as he attempted to politely refuse. I reminded him this was MY night, and he had to obey by MY rules. He held the cup up to his lips, and I tipped the bottom up for him, causing him to ingest a much larger drink than he had likely intended.

"Thatta boy!" I urged him.

A chick who was playing waitress in tattered jean shorts, suspenders, and a bra, approached the bar counter looking miserable. I beckoned her by snapping.

She turned her head in my direction. She had smokey makeup'd eyes and black lipstick against pale skin. A piercing through each side of her upper nose bridge glinted in the blacklight's faded glow.

"What do you want?" Her flat tone eradicated any sort of pleasantry.

"Can I get a few rounds of shots? Tequila if you have it?" Without acknowledgement of any kind, she grabbed four shot glasses and began filling. The amber liquid sloshed overtop the glass rims.

"Here." She slammed them down in front of us and I slipped her some bills.

"Cheers!" I sang out as I tipped my glass at him and tossed it back. He mimicked me and reluctantly threw his back as well while I slid another at him. He appeared disconcerted but swallowed that one as well. No salt or limes in this joint.

"Can we get this over with?"

He demanded rather rudely. I couldn't help but be a little vexed by his lack of manners. I didn't care under the terms he was here. It was still my night, and he had better deliver.

"Fine." I rolled my eyes and ambled down the hallway.

We passed a few open doorways, a red room and a blue room cast in the appointed colored lighting.

In each room we could see people blatantly having sex, out in the open. Swingers, furries, and orgy groups frequented the establishment. I'd done the swinger thing before, but furries and orgys hadn't really been my thing.

The red room showcased a queen bed with filthy stained sheets. Some chick who was shaved bald on one half of her head was leather strapped to the bed while a group of tweakers, hobos, and older men were jerking off surrounding her.

One senior was nailing her, and a guy who was clearly strung out was feeding his dick to her while he looked like he was seizing, staring at the popcorn ceiling.

The blue room featured a few hookers doing favors in exchange for blow and heroin. One guy was helping administer a needle between the web spaces of his partner's toes.

I knew Coach was likely ready to bolt after witnessing all this. Not his scene and I got that. I liked dirty places like this. The dirtier the better. Just a little secret fantasy of mine.

I peered over my shoulder to make sure he was still on my heels. Surprisingly, he was. A man of his word.

I finally found the room I was looking for. It was a bathroom, but not like what you'd expect in a typical house. It had been renovated in order to accommodate the high traffic demand the house often dealt with.

Homemade stalls had been assembled with old pallets screwed together, cardboard, scraps of plywood and such. It had one of those continuous towel roll dispensers in it, which no one in their right mind would ever use to wipe their hands, let alone anything else. Once blue, the cloth that was draped almost to the ground was a dingy gray and black with grime. I definitely noted some blood spattered on it as well.

In order to expand the bathroom, they had busted out one wall, and the bathroom meshed into the back alley. A dumpster lay against the fence and they had used some pvc pipes and leftover 2x4s to stake up some black poly around the area like walls.

I walked by the half smashed foggy mirror and double-checked my appearance. My medium champagne hair, that's what the box called it anyhow, was back brushed with my natural wave to give it some volume. I'd worn my cheetah print mini dress and hot pink bra that was peek-a-booing out the chest of my dress. It was a little ill fitted in the chest area since my boob job, but it gave the effect I liked, showing off my bust.

I had paired this hot little number with some red spiked heels that still didn't allow me enough height to stand eye to eye with Coach.

I had a session in the tanning bed that afternoon and had used one of my favorite tanning lotions. It had a slight orange tint that gave me a sunkissed glow.

My lips were painted with a hot pink lip stain, and I had applied blush to my cheeks. A bold eyeliner and, of course, my high volume mascara completed the look.

I took a moment to plump my breasts, hoisting them up in my bra, before guiding Coach into the only other stall with a real door.

"This is where you wanna do it?" He sneered.

"This is as good a place as any, unless you'd rather go join in on the red room?"

His eyes widened at my response, and he shut his mouth.

"Good. Now how about a bump?"

"A what?"

Oof, he was even more of a boy scout than I thought. I ignored his question, handed him my beer and produced a flap, a five dollar bill and credit card, from my bra. He watched, completely clueless.

The toilet was leaking all over around the base of the stool from their makeshift plumbing, and the linoleum was disintegrating. There was no toilet paper dispenser.

Making due, I dusted the grit off the top of the back of the toilet, unwrapped the flap and began cutting the powder. When it was ready I pivoted to face him.

"You ready?"

"For what exactly?"

I ignored him again. He asked too many questions.

I peeled off his shirt and started unzipping his jeans.

"Wait! Here?" He didn't even try to hide the repulsed tone to his voice.

"Yes, here. Got a problem?"

I lifted an eyebrow at him threateningly. He dismally shook his head as I tackled his fly.

I'd always wanted to do it in a dirty bathroom. Again, it fell in line with my little fantasy.

I yanked his pants and boxer briefs off his waist, disappointed to find him not even vaguely aroused. What a prick! Even if a dirty club bathroom wasn't his cup of tea, he had fucked mousey Connie no problem. I had at least worn my sexiest outfit!

I frowned at his limp crotch.

"Guess you need a little physical motivation."

He didn't respond.

"Well I have just the ticket!"

I quickly seized the prepped flap off the toilet and puffed my chest out, tapping a rail of white powder out across my tits. Rolling up the five dollar bill into a straw I handed it to him.

"What? No!" He backed up, finally clueing in.

"No isn't really an option here."

"I've never done drugs in my life!"

He protested adamantly.

"Well...not anymore!"

I pushed the straw into his hand while he looked at me in disbelief.

"You've gotten this far. Might as well."

I pushed again. It was fun, tainting his innocence. He looked pissed now and lowered my DIY straw onto the beginning of the rail I'd lined up for him.

I'd poured him more than I'd normally have given a first timer, just for the sheer fact that he was a big guy, and the fact that the more fucked up he was, the better time I'd likely have.

He snuffed it up and his eyes immediately closed with the burning sensation.

"Here." I said, as I raised my forefinger and plugged the one nostril.

"Suck in again." He obeyed.

"Good boy,"

I gave him a minute to bug out a bit while I pulled down the top of my dress and released *the girls*. Not wanting to waste an opportunity to show them off.

Once the clasps were released I could feel the weight of my tits as they flopped down, the bra no longer propping them up. I'd gone for a double D, heck why not? That was the point wasn't it? The bigger the better.

I waited patiently for the effect I was looking for but it didn't come as fast as I thought it would.

"Shit boy, you can't possibly have coke dick after one friggen bump!" I screamed at him.

He was holding his head and pacing the stall. I grabbed his ass cheeks and sat on the toilet's seat. If he wasn't going to naturally give me what I wanted, I'd have to work for it.

I grasped his still flaccid dick and began licking and sucking it. It took a few minutes, but no man can resist a blow job once it's commenced.

His member began to grow. My ex only had about four inches to work with. Coach had more than four inches on my ex. I found myself gagging more than I ever had previously in my lifetime. He tasted how he looked, with his yummy caramel skin. I wanted to devour him.

Now rock hard, I spit between my tits and squeezed his cock into my cleavage and set in motion titty fucking him. Sucking his tip with every other thrust. Clamping his throbbing meat between my breasts.

My areolas were bumpy with the thrill and the subtle breeze swooping under the stall door traveling from the lifting poly a few steps down.

The coke was working. His sensations were clearly heightened, and he was becoming hornier by the second.

He began gripping my head and forcing it down onto his knob, accelerating the pace that I had originally been keeping. His whole body was starting to twitch, his adrenaline ramping up. It was my turn.

I wiped the saliva off his shaft and told him to hold still. He was running his fingers through his hair, elbows straight up and his eyes wide, teeth gritted.

I grabbed the flap once more and poised another rail down his shaft. Rolling the five up again I stuffed it up a nostril and plugged the other, dragging and snorting every last spec.

"Whoa! That shit's pure as fuck!"

I'd have to tell my dealer how pleased I was with my recent purchase.

Coach was ready to fuck now. Standing there naked aside from his pants around his ankles, bobbing up and down like an Energizer bunny, on his toe tips.

I stood up, spun around to hand him my rear end, and he briskly reefed the material of my mini up. His hands automatically began searching for my undergarments in order to tug them off...but I wasn't wearing any.

"I saved you a step." I explained playfully.

The only response I got was a grunt before he pile drove his hog into me.

His hand grabbed my hip, and the other braced between my shoulders as he throttled into me again and again.

"Ooohhh fuuucckk yeah!" I screamed.

I must have startled the guy in the stall next to us who was passed out with a belt still around his forearm. I heard him stir, and his leg shot out under the barricade wall. Unphased, Coach barreled on.

My tits were flopping with each voracious thrust, again and again. I felt like my guts were being pushed through my abdomen wall.

Each push so forceful and so gratifying. Whoever said size doesn't matter, never fucked a dick over five inches, otherwise they would know...it matters!

I hiked my leg up, heel on the toilet seat, and stuck my ass out even more for him to be able to sink his prong in even further.

With one mighty heave, he did just that. Locating my button as he did.

I reached around behind me and grabbed his hands, pulling them up so he could hold my tits. I paid a hefty dollar for them. I wanted them to get the attention they deserved.

His palms bolstered them whilst his fingertips used my nipples as a grip strip. They became his handles, and he now used them to guide me back onto his dick, making me bounce on him.

With him now in my control, I pulled out my stripper skills from way back in the day, paying for college. I grinded down on him, weaving his cock up in me like a snake charmer commands a cobra to rise from its basket.

I unlocked and pushed open the stall door. Our reflection cast back at us in the cracked mirror. I wanted to watch!

My hips would go back, my chest would go forward. I could feel perspiration dripping off his forehead and falling on my lower back and asscheeks.

He wasn't going to be able to cum, I could tell that already. Oh well, I could and would, and it was really all about me anyhow.

I grabbed the flap again and took a small bump to elate me for the finish line. Coach didn't even pause his thrusting, he grabbed the flap out of my hand and took another snort himself.

"Look at you go!"

I couldn't help but comment. I wasn't even mad.

He pulled my leg down off the toilet lid and pushed me out of the stall bending me over the vanity.

I heard him hock a loogie of thick saliva and he spat it on my asshole. I didn't have a second to respond. He had pulled out of my box and stuffed it in my backdoor.

I sucked wind with pain, the first handful of pushes, I was paralyzed with agony. I was on the verge of cussing him out, when he hocked yet another loogie on his shaft and pushed in again. The extra saliva lubricated my rear and allowed me eased friction, and the prodding then turned from pain to pleasure.

I looked up, gaping at this hot young man, ass fucking me in a filthy club bathroom. I had to hand it to him. He'd really nailed my dirty fantasy!

My hands felt their way back and I pulled my cheeks apart and up, granting him more depth. He spat again and drove his meat in further.

Nothing went without feeling. Every plump vein protruding out of his shaft, each hard thrust, each gush of lady juice. I reached down through my wet muff of pubes and began to rub.

I wanted to orgasm! I'd never done it without vaginal penetration though. An empty beer bottle was left on the vanity . Getting creative, I lunged for it, rinsing it in the leaky tap. A handful of rubbers was lying on a soiled napkin in the center of the vanity as well. They'd been strategically placed in random areas throughout the building, including the coffee table, and bedside tables.

I reached for one of those too, ripping open the wrapper and gliding the latex material over the bottom of the bottle.

Using the neck of the bottle as a handle, I allowed my inner kink to really come out, relaxing and maneuvering it into my box. It was a hard angle to work while being bent over and butt-fucked simultaneously. But as soon as I got it in, it was worth it.

I grabbed his hand and wrapped his fingers around the bottle neck. My left hand went back to holding that side of my cheek out of the way while my dominant hand reached down again to *itch the ditch,* a term I had only recently heard it referred to as.

Watching in the mirror again, Coach exerted himself, pounding me hard and fast, all the while bottling my beaver. I kept squirting all over the bottle, and a puddle was running off it and Coach's knuckles onto the water damaged floor.

Macaroni plunger noises rang in my ears. Not usually what I would call a turn on, but since I was playing out a *dirty fantasy*, in this case it was.

"Fuck the shit right out of me!" I hollered.

My head turned in time to see an older man, late fifties, tall and slender, stall as he had been about to enter the doorway. Upon me seeing him, he paused to watch. Minutes passed by, and I allowed him the pleasure of observing, locking eye contact with him. His eyes bounced back and forth between me and Coach before he reverted back to casually walking back down the hall rather than piss whilst this carried on in front of him.

I started to see spots in front of my eyes, and the warm wave of an impending orgasm began to wash over me. I could hear myself moaning uncontrollably as Coach, on cue, barreled into my arse even more forcefully and frantically.

The warmth crept from my toes, up my calves and thighs, down from the tip of my nose to my loins in a feverish rush. Then I erupted.

One long elated moan bellowed out of me. Other party goers rushed to make sure no one was being murdered. But upon seeing me collapsed in ecstasy over the bathroom counter and a dick and bottle shoved inside me, they quickly returned to their own doings.

Coach wordlessly pulled out of my rear, and removed the bottle with a *pop* before pitching it in the trash can.

He moved to the double sink beside me and started washing up.

"We're even now. Deal's done."

He said as he wiped the sweat from his brow using his forearm.

"I suppose."

I shrugged coyly, still tingling in ecstasy and not wanting to come back down to reality.

"No, a deal is a deal. I've done my part. Now you do yours and hold your tongue."

I pouted my lip out at him as I began tucking my breasts away back into my bra.

"You don't want to make this a repeat thing?"

He couldn't have not had any fun at all? I wouldn't mind a few more rounds of this. I wanted to see if I could sway him.

He just looked at me, his brow furrowed, and an expression of disbelief adorned his face, before he hiked up his pants and walked out with his t-shirt still slung over his shoulder.

Guess not then.

"I'll see you next class!"

I called after him down the hall, and I couldn't help but smile.

10

Coach

I woke the next morning feeling more disgusted than I ever have before. Absolutely repulsed with myself. I showered twice and still felt revolting.

On top of feeling gross, my head was killing me. I couldn't blame the liquor as I had barely drank anything, I knew full well it was the coke...

God, I couldn't believe I'd done coke! I'd avoided hard drugs my whole life, so to cave now seemed so futile. I felt like a fraud; preaching good health and habits in my classes, then turning around and snorting shit up my nose.

I palmed my forehead. I'd definitely seen better days. Fucking Becky Carlyle probably ranked my second to worst night ever, but it was a close second.

She had better keep her damned mouth shut. Now that I thought about the whole reason I did what I did, I should've just let her spread her gossip.

People would either believe it or they wouldn't. The ones who stuck by me and continued to attend the gym, those were the kinds of people I wanted around anyways. Everybody else could fuck off.

But then I had to come back to the realization I had two mortgages, and every paid invoice at the end of the month mattered.

I didn't want any breakfast. The way I felt, I could go a week without eating. Thank goodness it was the weekend. I wasn't sure I could handle the noise or the rowdiness of a class today.

I flopped back down on my bed, burying my head in the pillows and pulling a blanket over my head. Within minutes I had drifted off.

Monday rolled around faster than I had the stamina for. Friday night was still vivid in my brain. I kept trying to force it from my memory and shake the fog, but it didn't seem to matter what I did. The memories and haze lingered.

If I sat still too long, manifestations of Becky's orange leathered skin and sun spots from her tanning bed would burn their way into the backs of my corneas. Cheetah print mini dresses, horrible boob jobs, no panties, and full afro bushes, ravaged my thoughts.

I did my best to keep myself busy. I couldn't help but go beet red when Connie walked in with Cooper that afternoon though. Connie seemed more than deflated when I didn't converse or hold eye contact with her.

I really did feel bad, but after what I'd done to safeguard both our reputations, I couldn't risk giving anyone a reason to look at us. Chalk it up to a one time thing and that's it.

I'd never intended to start a relationship anyhow. Unfortunately, I think perhaps that had been her hopes.

11

I had no idea what a hit the adult classes would be. I was surprised, Josh was right! A huge crowd showed up and continued in the weeks to come. Not just men either.

Women began coming more and more, balancing out the genders. It was a pleasant change of events. I was happy to see more females coming and empowering themselves, watching their confidence grow with each passing class.

One in particular caught my eye. Her skill level was unmatched. Her technique was explosive. Her name was Paige. She seemed so vaguely familiar, as if I'd met her in another life. But that was impossible.

She revealed to me that she kick boxed in high school. That made sense. She was tall, with an athletic girly build. She danced around her opponents like a boxer would, always remembering to keep her face protected.

I didn't want to single her out, using her as an example so often in order to demonstrate proper form to her classmates, but it was hard not to.

I had women on the sidelines watching me constantly, propositioning me. But once Paige joined my class, I suddenly felt guilty indulging in my sexual promiscuities.

She was the kind of fighter I needed on my competitive team. I couldn't be fooling around on the sidelines and coaching a future champ.

She didn't go unnoticed by the others in her class either. The women clearly felt intimidated and veered away from fighting her after the first few weeks. Realizing her skillset surpassed theirs undoubtedly.

The males viewed her in two different ways. I could hear all their sideline banter. To them she was a hot piece they'd love to sink their teeth into. However, they, like the females, were also intimidated. No one wanted to be beaten by a woman. They felt that would instantly make them look like jokes, and none of their egos could hold that weight.

It made her an outcast. But that seemed to suit her just fine. She kept to herself alot. She showed up alone. She was quiet and concise. Driven. She'd hit the bag, pelting it 'til it swayed this way and that with all her raw power and energy.

I had never felt so dumbfounded watching someone fight before. She rendered me useless. I wasn't aware what it was about her that caused me to lose my usual calm composure, but I didn't function the same when she was around.

One particular day I had instigated a pre-tournament sparring match, wanting to test their abilities in a real fight setting. Josh and his friends were all present and eager. They were all pairing up, and as usual, Paige was left on the sidelines. She paid it no heed and went to her usual corner to punch the bag some more.

The matches began and I talked the class through the moves as each group battled it out. The winners would go to one side, the losers to another, until the last partners went and the room was split, half and half.

Greg, one of the bigger guys in Josh's circle of friends, with a huge ego, was shit talking on the sidelines. I hated when guys got cocky. They'd under anticipate someone's skill level and would end up bloodied and broken after a fight. Greg needed to learn, be taken down a peg or two.

Paige was still off in the corner, working up a sweat. I announced that the winners would now compete with the partners I selected for them.

"Greg, front and center."

Greg stood up half laughing, looking around the room at his potential opponents.

"Who am I going to have to beat this round Coach?"

He clapped his hands, a sly smile escaping his lips as he viewed all the guys he'd just beaten.

"Paige!"

I summoned her from her corner. I could hear her fists stop hitting the bag, and she looked over at me with a suspicious unbelieving look in her eyes.

Greg laughed and sneered.

"Her? Coach, you have to be joking."

"I'm not at all, Greg. Why would you think that?"

"She's a woman! I'll obliterate her."

"I guess we'll see..."

Greg shrugged. His unfaltering confidence still unshaken.

"Bring it on." He beckoned.

His annoyance and arrogance rang clear in his tone. I could tell he wasn't going to go down without giving it his all.

Paige walked over, a bit at bay. Probably feeling a tad self-conscious at being made a spectacle. I had indeed put her on the spot, but this was the kind of pressure one would feel being in a champion fight. There was no easing you in, you had to jump in head first or be left ashore.

She wiped the sweat from her brow on a small towel she had next to her water bottle and approached the center of the mats where Greg awaited. He was puffing his chest and flexing, a pure intimidation strategy. I watched her eye him up, circling him slowly.

"Ok, clean match, shake and...begin!"

I had backed away allowing them their space. Greg, still viewing her like a joke, didn't even bother to raise his fists. He casually strode forward, waiting for her to make the first move.

Paige bobbed and weaved around him, fists up already, but she wasn't about to make the first move either. I could see, she had a plan. She licked her lips and anticipated his every move.

Greg finally broke, lunging at her. She dodged, dancing out of grasp with ease. Embarrassed, Greg's composure now appeared a bit shaken. He lunged again aiming to kick her legs out from under her.

Paige skipped over his legs and grasped his forearm sleeve, wrapping around his back and pinning his arm there, whilst simultaneously wrapping her other arm around his neck tight and pushing her toes into the backs of his knees. In one swift motion he was down.

I could see the embarrassment in his eyes, and the menacing anger. Not wanting to be outdone by a chick. Instead of tapping out, he used his hefty weight to slam down on her. Pinning forward at the waist, resisting her chokehold and flinging his body back against her, drilling her into the mat.

She clung on tight, squeezing his neck harder. His size and weight were his only weapons at this point, and she knew this. I didn't think she was about to give in to it. She was a fighter.

His face was beginning to purple. But he remained, heaving himself back, attempting to crush her, refusing to tap out. She squirmed and released her legs from under his body when he leaned forward pre-thrust. She wrapped them around his body and began squeezing her thighs around his diaphragm, locking her lower legs together so he couldn't break her hold. She was small in comparison to him, but she was all muscle, and she was crushing him.

Greg was struggling. His arms began to flail now, the lack of oxygen and pressure on his throat finally taking effect. His face turned from purple to a darkened stormy purple-gray. Veins popped out all over his forehead . His eyes now slits, he was digging his nails into her hands, trying by any means to break her grasp. He was playing dirty. She held steadfast.

That's when his body began to buckle and lurch. This idiot was going to let her choke him to death rather than tap out! I knew I had to step in and break it up.

"Ok, that's enough!" I announced,

Paige released him. His body went limp for a split second before his chest rose with a sharp inhale.

"That was a bullshit call, Coach." Greg's indignant voice rasped from the mat. Paige squirmed away from him, uncomfortable, clearly sensing this wasn't going to end peacefully.

"Seemed like an appropriate call to me. It was either that or you'd be leaving here in an ambulance."

"Fuck that!" Greg's voice rose angrily.

"Well, that's how it looked. She beat you fair and square. Let's not make a scene. These pre-tourney spars are also about showing your level of sportsmanship, you know. And if you're not going to be sportsmanlike, then I won't be taking you to the competitions and marring my gym's good name." I stated matter of factly.

"I'm creating champions here, not egotistical idiots who can't handle losing fair and square."

"Losing? I didn't tap out! I didn't lose!" He continued to argue.

"Would you like to take a vote? Who in this room thinks Greg lost?" I enquired.

"Show of hands." His classmates, looking increasingly uncomfortable, began to squirm. I knew they didn't want to single Greg out, especially with his temper on the rise, but there was no denying, Paige had won.

Josh stood up.

"Greg, c'mon man, just come sit down with us." I appreciated his efforts trying to keep the peace. Greg's face had turned from its faded purple tone to a bright rage infused and embarrassed red. He looked around at the class, and then at Josh.

"Fuck this!" He spat.

"Don't like it, you can leave, Greg." I motioned towards the doors. He met my gaze with a spiteful glare before he jumped up, snatched his water bottle and stormed off towards the changerooms.

Out of the corner of my eye I saw Paige shyly wriggle into the background, clearly upset that her one fight had caused such a scene. Her triumph had been trodden on by Greg's inflated male ego.

"Let this be a lesson to everyone here. I won't tolerate poor sports. We're supposed to celebrate each other's victories. As a team, each win is still a win. I won't stand for that kind of behavior. I want us to build each other up, not tear each other down."

With those final words, the mood shifted. Everyone nodded subtly, and I knew then, this was my group. We had weeded out the trash.

"Ok, let's go another round, partner up please."

Josh walked over as everyone paired up again and clapped a hand on my back, and I knew he was behind me one hundred percent.

Class ended and everyone cleared out. I grabbed my sanitizing solution and began wiping mats down as per my usual nightly routine. I thought I was alone when I heard a forlorn voice from behind me.

"Hey, Coach, I wanted to thank you for today. For giving me the chance to fight, and also for standing up for me afterwards."

It was Paige. I thought she'd left with the rest of the group, but I guess not. From her dampened hair, she must've had a shower prior to getting ready to depart.

"No need to thank me. You deserved a shot. I've been watching you. You've got talent, Paige. I'd like to see you paired up more often and actually get to use those skills. And you did NOT deserve Greg's attitude. I should be apologizing to you on his behalf for that ill display."

She hung her head shyly and shrugged her shoulders.

"I'm used to people treating me like that. Women think I'm too good, and men don't want to lose to the likes of me."

"Well, they have a reason to be scared." I winked at her playfully. I wanted to let her know, I saw her, saw how good she was. A small smile crossed her plump lips.

"I'd love to be able to spar more, just no one seems to want to."

"I'll see if I can work on that for you." I promised. I understood her frustration.

"What if..." she began.

"If?" I asked, unsure of her hesitation in her question.

"What if you sparred with me, Coach? I know it's not conventional, but you could teach me more things, take me under your wing. Then I'd have a partner, and maybe you could have your champion?" Her voice came out gruffer than usual, unsure, and panicked. Trying to spit everything she wanted to say in one long breath.

I thought for a moment.

"I don't usually spar with my students, especially not during class."

"I know..." her head hung.

"What if we did private lessons, after the adult classes?" Then it would be just me and you. I could give you the pointers you want and not be distracted from my other students?"

I was hoping she'd accept my compromise. It would mean even later nights for me, but I was willing to give up more sleep in exchange for having my champion fighter, and I knew she could go big.

"I don't know what to say...that would be amazing!" She smiled ecstatically.

"Perfect! It's a deal then. And in exchange, you'll compete for me?"

"Deal!" Her head nodded up and down frantically.

"So when do we start?" she asked.

I looked around, and gave the mat I was working on one final wipe.

"How about now?"

12

Her skills had progressed, far exceeding my expectations in the weeks we'd been training. Every Kamloops day I had, I stayed late working with Paige. I was tired, but I knew she was too, and it was going to be so worth it.

Our first competition together with her as my fighter was that coming weekend. It was a Thursday, and we were working our butts off getting her primed. She had stopped attending the adult classes. She would still show up and would work out while class went on, and then once everyone left, we'd commence her training.

"Ok, Coach, I need the real deal tonight. I want you to quit going easy on me."

"I haven't been going easy on you, I'm just preoccupied teaching you as we work."

"I know, but I need to practice like it's a real competition. No more coaching. Dish it out on me. Show me what I'll be up against."

She made a fair point. I wouldn't be doing her any favors not having her fully practice everything she'd learnt without my guidance. I needed to let her figure it out on her own.

"Alright... let's do this."

I turned up my music, as that's how I liked to work. A beat to drown out my brain, so I could focus completely.

Into It by *Chase Atlantic* came on, and I got into my ready position. Paige began circling me, like a tiger on the prowl, awaiting her kill. I stood in my ready stance and allowed her to do her thing. Closing my eyes and listening. I was a firm believer that you fight using all your senses.

She charged me. I heard the quickening swish of her gi come forth hard and fast. My hand shot out, catching her arm and maneuvering it around her back as I kicked her legs out from around her, taking her down in one motion. She looked surprised, clearly not expecting it.

I smiled at her, and she furrowed her brow at me. I wanted her to feel challenged; competitions weren't easy. This was her first taste.

With a burst of energy she broke my latch and scurried back up, ready for a second round. Her nostrils flared and eyes narrowed, pouncing at me. A foot came out locking between my legs, and a fist gripped my gi collar whilst another latched onto my sleeve.

I anticipated her move and stepped backwards over her leg then did what I refer to as a "misdirection" move. She still had my gi gripped tight, but I came into her, stepping past her back, and used my hand closest to hers to grab the arm she had my sleeve gripped with. She was now in an awkward position with the one arm she was gripping my chest with pinned and the other locked on my arm. I had the perfect opportunity. I spun around and in one move lifted both her elbows up, bending her arms the opposite direction they're usually meant to go in, thus breaking her grip on me.

From there I quickly maneuvered one leg around over top of her dominant leg, grabbed her collar, stuck my rear into her waistline pitching forward and slung her over my body onto the ground, mounting her before she could make any moves.

She was both surprised and angry. I could see her temper rising. She had a competitive heart and by no means enjoyed being beaten so easily.

She bucked her hips up forcefully, giving her enough leeway to bring her knees up. She was flexible enough she pulled and rolled her knees up through my legs and wrapped them around my neck and once again grasped my collar.

I had really only one move, and that was to try to break her grip. That proved to be harder to do than I thought.

Her grip was deadlocked. Her anger fuelled her strength. I felt her thighs tightening around my neck. In any other situation I would have killed to be in this position with a girl as stunning as Paige. The heat of her loins radiating off my face, the scent of her pheromones intoxicating me.

What was I thinking? She was my student. I couldn't deny my attraction to her, but I had to keep my professionalism. It was one thing dipping into the mom pool, but quite another to be into one of my students. It was inappropriate. I had to shake my head, trying to keep my thoughts in check.

Realizing she had me, she pulled down hard on my gi collar which then slid my neck deeper into the depths of her groins and she squeezed her thighs harder. Her calves locked behind my back and pulled me into her. I didn't see any way out, my brain was blurry with lack of oxygen and effort to wrestle both her and my ever growing erotic thoughts. Trying and failing to keep them at bay.

I tapped out.

Unlocking her legs, she stood up looking very smug indeed. Instead of breaking for water, she crouched again, ready once more.

This girl is insatiable! I thought, knowing full well, I was even more intrigued.

We both attacked simultaneously. It became a bear wrestle, and we relied on our legs to do most of the fighting for us. Battling it out to be the first to take the other down.

Being in such close proximity, our bodies worked hard. The sweat began to roll, beads forming on our foreheads. Our breaths came out in labored puffs. Our legs finally tangled, and we went down, forming a heap on the gym mats. The air was muggy as we battled it out. Rolling, clawing at each other's arms to break grips. Legs and feet squealed on the rubber beneath us as we drug our bodies across the mats.

I managed to wrap my legs around her waist, and she rolled atop me with my gi in her fists. I had the shoulders of her gi locked in mine as well. She looked down at me, her eyes still narrowed slits, her brow furrowed and jaw clenched.

I could feel her drag herself into a kneeling position, and I squeezed my legs around her tighter which pulled her body and face down closer to mine. Her face hovered just above my chin. We held our positions. Locked in place. Sweating and panting. Grunting with exhaustion. That's when she did the unexpected.

She used all her strength to pull at my gi, stretching the material outwards off my body. My belt had fallen loose and with that extra pull fell completely off, hitting the mat with a subtle *thud*.

She stared at me glaring, analyzing me. Then she gave her body a thrust from the knees up, propelling her face forward. Her lips locked on mine.

She held them there, waiting for me to do something. Accept or reject. I was stunned.

I shouldn't.

But she was making it very hard to refuse. Her hands released my gi, and she slipped them behind my head. She pulled me even tighter into her, forcing my lips open to receive her. I gave in.

Passions ran high. We kissed. And oh what a kiss! Fiery and hot! She tasted like salted vanilla caramels, sweet and savory. I loosened my leg lock, and she climbed up and over onto my lap, undoing her own gi top and tossing it aside whilst still kissing me, not wanting to part for even a single second.

Our sweaty bodies intertwined, she pinned my hands down, leaning over me, kissing me intensely. My erection at full mast, plastered against my pants.

She continued to hold me down and started kissing my neck and chest, working her way down to my drawstring, untying it while subtly kissing my pantline.

As soon as I felt the tension release from my pants, I lifted my hips, and she tore them and my undergarments off my body with a ferocity unmatched by any woman I had ever been with before. I sat up pulling at her top, kissing her, wanting to feel her skin on mine. I peeled each arm off and then lifted her sports bra over her head.

Her tanned brown skin accentuated her muscular physique. Her tangled braid hung over one shoulder, and loose hair stuck to her back and chest. Caught up in the clamminess of her sweat soaked skin, I couldn't help but admire her beauty - no makeup, sweat, messy hair, nothing took away from it. In fact, I think she was even more stunning because of it.

I pulled her back towards me, feeling her body press into mine. Her bare chest on mine, our hearts were beating rapidly. Our hands interlocked, and that was it.

I wanted her! No, I *needed* her.

I grabbed behind the small of her back and flipped her over, kissing down her body like she did mine. I admired every detail as I worked my way down her body. She stretched up, elongating her stomach, giving me more area to kiss. Massaging her breasts all the while, I tugged at her pants, and she allowed me to pull them off.

I bit the hem of her panties and pulled them down with my teeth, inhaling her seductive scent.

An upside down teardrop of well trimmed pubic hair was the only thing left on her body. I looked her up and down, my cock rigid with want. *How could I be so lucky?*

I kissed down her body all the way to her pubis. I'd never recalled being so hungry to eat pussy before in all my life!

She didn't play shy. As soon as she felt my lips on her labia, her hips thrust up, pushing my face into her crotch right where I wanted to be. I licked, circling her pearl before sliding down her slit and back up and around. Finding my rhythm. Engulfing her pussy with my mouth.

Her moans of approval sent shivers up my spine. She entangled her fingers in my hair, clawing my scalp and shoving me deeper into her honeypot. Her back arched and her knees splayed open. I wanted to watch her.

Her eyes closed, she was biting her bottom lip, exuding her pleasure. I slipped a finger up in her while I licked on. Her tight wet clam squeezed my finger. I slurped her tangy juices that gushed over my knuckle. Good to the last drop, then I'd make her gush more.

She swung her knees up over my shoulders, and I crawled in even further. Deep fucking her with my finger and lapping at her clit fiercely, pausing only to use my tongue as extra girth for my finger. I'd stick my tongue alongside my finger and swipe around it as I pushed up in her, sliding my tongue deeper and deeper. Stretching her gently.

Her clit was swollen and ripe. She squirmed uncontrollably with even the slightest touch of my tongue or feeling my hot breath.

She was ready.

I crawled up her body, and she pulled at my shoulders, indicating her desire. We locked lips again, let her taste herself on my lips, a flavor I wouldn't soon forget. I wanted to savor it and its sticky, brown-sugary goodness.

My cock throbbed with eagerness. Pre-cum flowed from its tip as a precursor to the task of easing myself in without causing discomfort.

Our chests pressed together, and I searched her eyes for consent. I'd never been so hesitant to enter into a sexual relationship before; but something about Paige was different, I could feel it.

She returned my gaze and sucked that big bottom lip of hers. She gave a nod. I lined up my dick with her entrance and gave a small push.

The warmth and wet that was emitting from her hit my dick like a tidal wave. Her cavern collapsed in on me, squeezing me as I pushed in further and further. I wanted my full length in her. We both gasped as my balls hit her ass and I reached that internal magical spot.

I paused, wanting to give her a moment to break in around me. She breathed through it, panting in my ear. She sucked my ear lobe when she was ready for me to move. Small, short thrusts allowed her to stretch out around me.

Her legs wrapped around me, she began rocking them when she was ready for more, pulling me into her.

My prick tingled with each thrust in, feeling her hot juices jet over him. The wetter she got, the more she wanted. I thought back to my initial thought about her... Insatiable!

She grabbed my neck and pulled herself up onto my lap. I rocked back onto my knees, and she began riding me.

Her perky tits bounced off her chest as she drilled my dick into her as far as she could take it. She wasn't being quiet anymore. Neither was I. Our moans, groans, and her shrieks echoed throughout the gym. If it wasn't for the music still playing in the background I'm sure a passerby would've called the cops.

It wasn't long before we were covered in another layer of perspiration; sweat had never turned me on so much before in my life. I'd always want to shower, but now I didn't give two shits. I wanted the sweat to pour.

She bucked harder and harder, and I thrusted, kick standing her as she bobbed up and down until I finally lowered her so she could buck some more.

I slid my hand up her thigh, over her ass and up her back, mapping out her body. Felt her goose pimples rise up from the sensation of it, my hand damp with her gloss.

She ground down on me, corkscrewing my cock into her. Then she lifted her left leg up and over my head, turning herself around while still perched on my lap.

I grabbed her braid with one hand and her ass with the other and began drilling her. I watched my dick slam in and out of her. Her butt jiggling on impact. Her curtains parting around my veiny girth. I loved seeing her squirt with every deep thrust in.

I pulled her braid back, forcing her to arc her back even more. I pulled her up so I could kiss her neck and taste her skin again. Her weight shifted and settled down and my dick sunk in a few more centimeters. We both felt it.

Her pussy instantly clamped around the base of my cock and I humped harder, the pressure building.

Keeping a hold of her braid I let go of her ass and reached around, feeling her breasts before I lowered my fingers and rubbed her wet button.

That was the last motion she needed to put her over the edge. Within seconds, her body was shuddering and her breaths coming out in fast gasps.

Instinctively, I began slamming my hips into her, ready to bust. I was more animal than man at that moment.

Her walls enclosed around me, choke holding my dick. Her howls bounced off the walls, and I let go.

Pulling out, I almost didn't make it. Hot creamy jizz poured from my cock glazing her ass cheeks like frosted cinnamon buns. My moan ended in a gruff grunt, exulting our activities.

We flopped into each other's arms on the damp and sticky mat. We just laid there exchanging body heat and stroking each other sensually. I knew right then, this was what my life had been missing. Actually not this...her.

12.5

Paige

I'd been working one on one with Coach for a few months since the altercation with Greg. I felt stronger. I knew my skill set had expanded exponentially, but that wasn't the only thing that had grown. I couldn't help but feel more than just the admiration most students feel for their teachers. There was something about him. I couldn't put my finger on it. I felt comfortable in his presence, secure, and knew he only wanted what was best for me. He was good looking, and the more hands on work we did, the more I wanted my hands on him.

I'd never felt this way before with any man. It wasn't just the adrenaline pumping through my veins making my heart palpate faster and harder during our evening grapples. It wasn't just the high energy sparring we did battling for mount that caused perspiration to roll off our bodies. And it wasn't just the late summer mugginess in the gym causing my loins to go aflame.

I made my move one night during a session. I couldn't handle it anymore, the suspense, the want, the building desire. I felt something for him. I knew so little about him, and yet felt our souls connect in some way. I wanted to explore that, get closer; he had to feel it too.

Thankfully, he returned my passion and we made love right there on the gym mats. Normally I'd just say we fucked, but this was more; and I knew it.

I wasn't sure where to go from there though. Was I his girlfriend? Still his student? A side piece? The way he caressed me afterwards, I had to believe there was more to it. I meant more to him. But I needed confirmation. I'd be his fighter regardless, but I didn't want to miss an opportunity for the real thing either. I was done with boys; I wanted a man.

My first competitive fight was that weekend. I was as ready as I was ever going to be. Coach and I decided to carpool together to the tournament in Red Deer, Alberta. It would be a long drive. He was going to do the majority of the driving, so I could rest up but could take shifts with him.

I was nervous for the fight as well as being in such close quarters with Coach for such an extensive period of time. Especially after our rendezvous just the evening before. It was Friday morning early, and he had called to let me know he was fueling up and then would be enroute to my place to pick me up.

He had brought me a tournament gi so I only had to pack my casual attire and necessities. I jumped in his truck as he pulled up, and he handed me a tea.

"Thank you."

I'm not sure how he knew I was more of a tea person than coffee, but was pleased I didn't have to disappoint him with that news had he handed me the dark bitter beverage.

I gave a sniff, he had even guessed my favorite flavor; vanilla Chai. He just smiled at me in return, happy that I was happy.

I thought the drive would be awkward, but it wasn't. We talked, told stories, laughed, even the rare silent moments were comfortable.

He had closed the gyms with plenty of notice for the tournament that weekend. Josh Davis and a few of kids and teens. We would all be representing BJJ-Wild Dogs and I think we all wanted to give it a good reputation. I knew he was hoping for that. This was his way of getting his gym's name out there, having us do well. I wanted to be the one to do that for him. Be his champion.

The first match would be Saturday morning. We had left on Friday in order to make sure we wouldn't be late if any unexpected road closures were to occur, and so we could rest before the matches.

Coach had taken the liberty of renting us a motel room for the night in Red Deer, with two queens and a kitchenette. I think he opted for the two queens as a courtesy, thinking maybe I'd want my own bed. It was a cute notion, but I knew I couldn't wait to melt into his body again that night.

The eight and a half hour drive was a test of my restraint. It was hard to keep my hands to myself. I think he was struggling as well. I noticed his hand creeping across the seat towards my hand countless times, wanting so badly for our fingers to touch, before he'd reel it back in. Clearly re-thinking his actions, not sure where he stood with me.

I wanted to tell him, wanted to reach for his hand and let his big palms engulf mine, but I too was hesitant. It was only my first tournament. I didn't think either of us wanted to present like we were together. It could be so easily misconstrued into something it wasn't; some kind of advantage.

When we pulled into the motel that night, it was such a relief to stand and stretch. Coach checked in, and we hauled our bags up.

Slipping the key in the door, he gave it a turn and pushed his way into the darkened room. I was about to follow when I heard my name being called from a few doors down.

"Paige?"

I turned in the direction of the voice. It was Pam, another woman I knew from the gym.

"I should have known you'd be competing. We should have driven together! Tara and Giselle are here too; they're just checking out the pool. Hey, you should just stay in our room with us! We never really get to see you at class anymore. It would be nice to get to know you, build that team spirit. What do you say?"

I stood there, a bit flabbergasted. Coach was hidden within the doorway, and we were both holding our breath. She hadn't seen him, just me. Our cover wasn't blown, but I wasn't sure how I was going to get out of this.

"Well, I already rented the room." I motioned towards the door.

"Oh, you haven't even stepped in it yet I'm sure they'd refund you no problem. Come on, I'll walk down with you."

She beckoned to me and began walking down the hall towards the elevator. Shit. I'm not sure why now, of all times, they all of a sudden cared to extend their hand of friendship. I'd been alone at the gym for how long now with not so much as a "Hello Paige." And now they wanted to be roomies? I looked at Coach pleadingly. I didn't know what to do. I didn't want to stay with those women. I wanted to be with him, but I knew neither of us wanted our new relationship to be exposed either. His eyes looked sad, but he gave me a nod indicating I should go. I reluctantly grabbed the knob and pulled the door closed once more. Following Pam down the hall, I knew I'd have to just pretend to check out so Coach would have a place to sleep.

Timing was on my side as Tara and Giselle were on their way back from the pool as Pam and I exited the elevator. She explained she'd invited me to join them for the night while I walked over to fake my checkout. I instead asked the receptionist a silly question about where I could purchase some new boxing gloves. She kindly drew me a map and gave me directions. Her attention to detail made my fake checkout seem more plausible, and I joined the ladies further back in the lobby moments later.

I wasn't sure how overly ecstatic Tara and Giselle were about having me accompany them, but Pam was so chatty no one had a second to get a word in edgewise if they were to protest. I trailed them back to their room and finally set my bags down. Pam and I would be sharing a bed. I opted for the pullout couch, but she insisted.

There was a Dennys down the street, and we walked there for dinner. I'd have given anything to instead be ordering food into the motel room with Coach. Yet there I was one of the gang all of a sudden, much to my dismay. I'd longed for that sort of kindness for months, and gotten nothing but sneers and distance. Now, at the worst possible moment, they decided they wanted to give me a shot.

Pam insisted we order some drinks with our meals. I was skeptical if we should have even been drinking prior to a match the next day. But again, there was no arguing with Pam. I sipped my beer as they sucked back their daiquiris and cocktails. I was trying my best to be friendly and carry on the conversation, but I kept resorting back to my quiet reservedness. Tara finally couldn't hold her tongue and cut Pam off, bringing my attention back.

"So Paige, you've been doing private training classes with Coach? How's that been?"

She sucked on her straw a little more suggestively than I would have liked, smiling all the while.

"Uh, it's been fine. Nice to learn one on one and have that guidance."

I shrugged, trying to appear nonchalant. They weren't about to give up that easily. They all jumped in, digging for more information.

"So you're just alone with Coach for the entire time?" Giselle inquired.

"How do you keep your hands off of him?" Pam screeched.

"Does she though?" Tara implied.

They sat there awaiting my responses. I didn't know what I could safely divulge that would appease their thirst for gossip but wouldn't get twisted into something more.

"Yes, it's just the two of us. It can be pretty grueling, he trains me hard. He is very professional. I won't lie, I find him attractive, but he's my Coach; some lines shouldn't be crossed."

I lied, but only slightly.

They seemed disappointed with my answer. Tara scoffed.

"What a waste of a perfectly good opportunity." She rolled her eyes and commenced sucking on her straw.

The other two heaved big sighs, their shoulders slumping.

"We were hoping to hear some sexy details to add to our fantasies, oh well." Pam explained.

I felt increasingly uncomfortable following. Thank goodness the waitress came with our food, and the sound of our chewing filled the awkward silence that befell the table.

Crawling in bed with Pam that night, I felt nothing but resentment. I wished for any excuse to leave and return to Coach's room. Instead I was being robbed of my time with him by women who all just wanted to live their sick pipe dreams vicariously through me. They didn't want to be my friends. They just wanted information. I didn't give them what they wanted, and now I was reduced back to nothing in their eyes. Back to exile.

13
Coach

The alarm woke me with its blaring radio. I had spent the night alone. Paige had been drug away by Pam, another one of my adult students. She hadn't realized I was already in the room Paige was entering. For that I was grateful, as well as for Paige's discretion in the matter.

I couldn't help but feel a strong animosity towards Pam in that moment though. I had been looking forward to that time with Paige, alone. I was hoping to connect with her more, I'd never felt so close to someone before. I wanted to build on that. Last night would have been a great opportunity to do just that, but I was denied the chance.

Perhaps I was being selfish. This could be Paige's opportunity to finally make some peer friends in the gym. I shouldn't trump on that. Friends would be good for her.

I yawned and stretched. I at least had the tournament to occupy my thoughts today. I was all nerves. I could only imagine how Paige felt.

I pulled into the arena's parking lot. The sea of vehicles made it difficult to locate a spot, even with my early attendance. I managed to find a spot, cranking my tires into the tight space. Hopping out, I slung my bag of gear over my shoulder and strode towards the entranceway. I hoped my fighters would all arrive early so I could get them warmed up and give them the low down on the rules and etiquette.

I walked to the table and signed in. I had pre-registered all my fighters, and they had appointed us a changeroom and a corner in the gym. The volunteer heading the table gave me the run down and a schedule that accounted for each round, the times, which rings, and what numbers each fighter was listed as. She handed me a stack of liability waivers to disperse amongst my group and a handful of pens. I thanked her and headed in the direction of our changeroom to get set up.

Within the half hour, my group had all shown up. Paige accompanied by Pam, Tara, and Giselle, all of whom seemed far less friendly than usual. I directed them all to change after handing out the BJJ-WD competition gis I had ordered for them all. When you entered a tournament, you needed your team to look sharp. They were representing you and your image.

They emerged from the changeroom looking sharp as hell in their crisp new linens with my logo emblem embroidered on them. We huddled together on the portion of the arena designated to our group and organized our stuff while I announced my plans to them.

"Okay guys, we're going to run a few laps, then do a quick warm up and stretches. Fights are set to start in the next twenty minutes. You guys are going to do great. Let's do this!"

With that note, I gave my signature clap, all their hands clapping along with mine, then we took off. I led the pack and they all followed. I wanted their blood pumping, wanted them warm. No injuries that could be avoided were going to happen. Around and around we went.

When our warm up was done, I could see the flush in all their cheeks. They were primed and ready for action.

Kids were to start. I led them over to their section and waited for their numbers to be called.

One by one, my fighters all took their turn. Many came up victorious. I could see the other coaches leering over at our quadrant. We had walked in the underdogs. No one knew our name, and yet they saw us walking away with all golds and silvers.

Paige had been keeping to herself, doing her usual warm up routines or watching as the teens and men took their turns. I could see her eyes flicking back and forth, anticipating their moves. She was planning her moves like any true fighter would.

It was getting later in the day, and it was finally the ladies time to battle it out. Pam was up first.

She was defeated, an unfortunate loss for us. Giselle was next up. It was a rocky spar, both competitors struggled through each round. The ref eventually called it a tie. Tara's turn came next. I didn't have much hope. She didn't attend regularly enough and had an arrogant air about her.

My intuition was right. She didn't have the stamina. I saw her faltering from the sidelines. Her breaths heaved with exhaustion. She must have known she wasn't going to make it. She started playing dirty. I saw the illegal finger lock she tried on her opponent when she was down and they had mounted her. The ref called it too.

The Ref hollered for a time-out, escorted her off the mat and gave her and me a stern warning. I took the opportunity to give her my own warning as well.

"If I catch you doing any more illegal moves, you're done, I'll call the fight. I can't have you winning like that. We can't fear loss when it's a fair loss. If you're not ready, you're not ready. We'll get them next time. You understand me?"

She looked pissed, glaring at me, but nodded and ambled back out onto the floor. The ref motioned and the fight started up again.

It was only seconds in and I saw it again. She was fighting dirty. She tried to fish hook her opponent's mouth after a bad roll. She could have broken her opponent's arm with that roll, and the fish hook wasn't a move at all. That was just plain dishonorable fighting.

I motioned to the referee and he approached me.

"We're calling it." I said.

"You're sure?" He questioned, eyebrow raised. He clearly hadn't seen the foul moves I had.

There weren't too many coaches that would forfeit based on their own competitor's behavior.

"Yes, I'm sure. She was warned. She needs to learn this isn't what my team is about. Call it."

"Alright."

The ref jogged back to the middle of the mat and partitioned the two sweaty competitors, lifting their arms into the air.

"Brazilian Jiu-Jitsu Wild Dogs forfeit." He announced, his voice bellowing over the loudspeaker.

Tara's eyes darted in my direction, narrowing into piercing slits. I had warned her.

She stormed off the mats, grabbed her stuff and fled. I imagined it must be pretty embarrassing for her to have her own coach forfeit a fight due to her poor conduct. She'd made it clear that she didn't understand that it was embarrassing for my gym, for our team, to have someone either win under false pretenses or to fight dirty. It just wasn't respectable and I couldn't condone it.

At Tara's departure, I could see Pam and Giselle out of my peripherals grouping together, glowering at me and whispering in hushed tones. As far as I was concerned, they could whisper all they wanted. It wouldn't change my mind. A poor sportsman is a bad sportsman, and I didn't want that on my team.

A few more matches went on between the other teams before Paige's number was called. This was it, the fight I'd been waiting for.

Paige had been apprehensively pacing our area up and down until she heard her number called. Hearing the booming voice over the loudspeaker call out her name stopped her dead in her tracks. I noted her face had a whitish pallor. Her nerves were getting the better of her.

"You'll be fine. Get out there and show 'em what you're made of." I growled at her.

She looked at my face and I nodded reassuringly. I knew she could do it. Her confidence lifted, and I saw her jaw set, determined as she strode towards the center of the mat.

"For Kootenay Regional BJJ Cougars number eleven, we have the illustrious Cathy or "Cat" Burgess." The loudspeaker announced. A roar of applause followed.

"Her counterpart this evening, number seventeen, the Brazilian Jiu-Jitsu Wild Dogs, Paige Bryant."

Both women stepped forward to clap hands and agree to a fair fight. To say Cat Burgess had an advantage in this fight would have been an understatement. Her broad shoulders and muscular build in addition to her height made Paige look tiny in comparison. Paige was 5'9" which made her tall for a woman by most standards, but Cat had her beat. She must have measured in around 5'10" maybe even 5'11". Her hair was braided in tiny corn rows across her scalp. Her teeth were bared, showing off her artfully blood spattered design mouthguard.

Cat Burgess was well known at these tournaments. I'd heard her name being tossed around the arena and had overheard a few of the other coaches talking.

"Cat Burgess is here, going to be one hell of a show."

"Isn't she undefeated in her last five fights?"

"I believe so. She took an injury in her last one though, tore a ligament in her shoulder I believe. She's been off for a while."

"Still, she'll do well here. Probably leave here with another gold."

"You can bet on that."

I'd heard all I needed to. I had to admit, I had more than enough confidence in Paige. I mean she could take on me, a full grown man with many title championships under my belt, and damn near win. But alas, this Cathy Burgess had me worried. I knew she could be quite aggressive, and she had tons of experience. Her previous injury could give us a helping hand, but that's not how I wanted us to win. I just hoped Paige could keep her wits about her and take the heat I knew Cathy would be bringing.

Their palms clapped and the fight was initiated. Cat stepped forward into Paige's airspace. Clearly she would be the instigator of the battle. Paige danced about her, returning to her boxing habits, which I hoped would serve her well.

Cat kept reaching for Paige's gi, but Paige slapped her hand away again and again. You could see Cathy's annoyance building; her temper rising.

With a solid lunge she managed to grasp Paige's collar, planted the sole of her foot against her hip then threw herself to the ground launching Paige down with her. Paige was quick though and swiftly rolled to her knees, and just missed Cat's attempt to mount her.

Cat charged her again. She wanted to take her down to the mat where she knew she could finish her off quickly. Paige deflected her charge with an almighty heave, but Cathy managed to grasp her sleeve. She yanked her into her clutches and sought to bear wrestle her to the mat, which she inevitably did. Her strength overpowered Paige's own. It wasn't looking good.

They grappled on the floor for a bit. Paige had her in her guard. I could make out Paige's attempt to kimura Cat's arm but Cathy saw it coming and managed to snake her arm out of it, breaking her arm lock. Cathy stood up, and Paige managed to clutch her gi collar as she did so and saw her opportunity; she went for it. In the blink of any eye, she swung her left foot up and pinned it against Cat's right hip, then grasped her right arm sleeve. Her right leg and foot raised up onto Cat's left shoulder. She pulled Cat's upper body down towards her and then slid her hand from the collar down to lock her wrist as she simultaneously lifted her hips and turned into Cathy's forearm. She arm barred her in that instant.

Cat was forced to yell.

"Tap!"

Her face did not hide the shock she felt having an amateur quash her winning streak.

13.5

Paige

My utter bafflement could not have been hidden even if I had tried. I had won my first fight! Against none other than Cat Burgess, of all people. I'm not even sure how we had managed to get paired together given her level of experience. But I guess my height was likely a factor. There weren't too many women as tall as me. My aunts had always told my mother I should be a model. I'm sure my mother likely would have pursued it too, had I not made my preferences for sports and *boyish* activities well known. She'd always fuss and nag me.

"Honey, do something with your hair. There are girls who would absolutely kill for hair like yours, and you can't even be bothered to brush it."

"Why don't you wear a dress? For goodness sake child, we're going to the church social. What will the Pastor think?"

My response was always an eye roll or a sarcastic comment of some sort which only further irritated her. She quite often dismissed me; couldn't be bothered. She preferred to instead spend time with my older sister. My sister Lori was kind to me; she sympathized with me for the way my mother chose not to care just because she couldn't relate to me. We were close, and I was thankful for her allowing my mom to fuss over her more in an effort to take the heat off of me.

Shaking the thoughts from my head, I walked over to the Wild Dogs area to join my team mates. Coach greeted me with an enthusiastic hug and clap on the back, but as for the rest of them... As always, they glowered at me from their spots, not moving. Josh Davis came over and paid his respects with a firm handshake and a smile. He was a nice dude; I could see why Coach liked him.

"Great job out there. Cat is not an easy opponent to take on." He affirmed.

I couldn't agree with him more.

We each fought two fights that day. My next opponent wasn't as challenging as Cathy Burgess and was a much easier take down, which I was kind of relieved about. My adrenaline was still pumping from that first undertaking. I Ezekiel-choked her in the first minute; short but sweet.

After a few more fights, they held an award ceremony front and center. They called names and would award medals. Everyone on our team managed to acquire a medal, all golds and silvers and only one bronze. It was a victorious first tournament for the club. Coach was glowing, beaming with pride at every one of us and congratulating us all.

Pam and Giselle had to catch up to Tara, who had gone back to the motel. Giselle convinced her over a phone call to come back to pick them up so they could hit the road home. I picked up on the fact that I was no longer included in their plans and received no invitation for a ride home. That suited me better anyhow. In fact, I was more than pleased.

Coach saw all his team off on the road before wiping down and packing up the gear into the back of his truck. That's where he found me waiting.

"I wasn't sure if you'd gone back with the ladies or not."

He gave me a questioning look. He must have sensed that things had gone awry. There was no way he had missed the tension between us all.

"Not on your friggen life would I be driving eight and a half hours with those cranky ol' biddies." I half joked.

In all actuality, it was mostly honesty. I'm sure he read between the lines though.

"I take it your night wasn't as enjoyable as it should have been?"

"You got that right. All they wanted was the low down on you. Smutty details. I don't shit where I eat. They didn't care much for my lack of details." I shrugged.

His eyes looked apologetic.

"I'm sorry. I'm already causing problems for you."

"What? No! These problems existed long before you. I've always been an outcast, always will. This is nothing new. Please don't blame yourself."

I didn't want him to think he was causing me any more issues. Women always treated me poorly, Lori always insisted they were jealous. I just figured they couldn't handle the fact that someone of their same gender got along better with males than they did. I didn't really, though I used to.

I used to have lots of guy friends, but now that I was a woman, guys wanted to date me; which I wasn't usually interested in. And then when I rejected them, all of a sudden I was the enemy. I then became the topic of their negative banter. If I also happened to beat them at sports, deadlifts, or any of the activities males usually excel in. Then I was really disliked.

To men, I was just an object. I wasn't a person. I'd been called a *hot piece* too many times before. No regards for my personality, my likes or dislikes, nothing. I was just something they wanted to stick their dick into, that's it. I had grown to resent men because of it.

But Coach was different. He liked that I enjoyed fighting. He wasn't focused just on my looks, he wanted to get to know me better. He noticed me, all of me. And he wanted me to succeed. For the first time in a long time, a man had piqued my interest.

"Forget them, let's go celebrate. I'm hungry!" I grinned, whilst tossing my hair back over my shoulder.

"Yeah, I bet you are. You deserve a good meal after competing the way you did today!" Coach's approval was written all over his face.

"You better believe it! Let's go!"

I grabbed the handle of his truck, and he unlocked it to allow me in before walking around to his side and climbing in next to me.

We drove around and came across some kind of street event or celebration. One street was closed down to traffic. Food trucks were parked up and down the street along with pop up tents, vendors, and show cars. It reminded me of the annual Hot Night in the City event that Kamloops held. Live music played from bands positioned just out of ears' length of each other. Fairy lights were strung lamppost to lamppost lighting the street up.

"Oooo, can we stop here?" I begged.

"I guess this is as good a spot as any." He agreed with a smirk.

We walked up and down the street, checking out all the stands and the vendors' merchandise, all the while keeping an eye out for the food truck that intrigued us the most. We eventually settled on fish tacos and some ice cold Coronas with limes. I'd never imagined that our night would turn into a date, but it indeed had.

The sun had almost completely disappeared, just a blanket of blazing red and orange sinking behind the buildings remained. The music from the band closest to us filtered around my ears. I wasn't much of a dancer, but heck, I figured we were celebrating.

"Let's dance!"

I jumped up from our tiny deli table and grabbed his hand, guiding him out into the street where a crowd had formed swaying and dancing to the music. I could feel his reluctance, his weight still planted in his seat. I looked at him, stuck my bottom lip out at him and gave him puppy dog eyes. He heaved himself up with a long winded sigh.

"I guess, this is your night..."

I squealed my excitement. I wasn't usually a squealer either, but it was hard to contain myself. I'd won gold that day and had a night with Coach all to myself.

I spun around to face him again and tugged him into me close. I could sense that he wasn't sure if he was comfortable or not being out in public with me, even though we were in a city far from prying eyes and rumors. I placed his hands on my hips and wrapped my arms around his neck, making him sway with me. He looked around restlessly, I took my one hand and tipped his chin back to face me; forced him to lock eyes with me.

He gazed into my eyes and I into his. I didn't even want to blink. I was afraid if I did, I'd end up waking up in my bed back in Kamloops. I noted he wasn't blinking either. His expression soft, thoughtful, and content.

The music played on, and we continued to sway, mesmerized in each other's gaze. The heat of the night air enveloping us, I lost myself in his embrace. His big hands softened, no longer tense. He swiftly brushed a tendril of hair from my face. His fingers hesitated by my chin. Reading his mind, I tiptoed up, smooshing my lips into his. We both held them there, neither of us wanting to be the first to pull away. I opened my mouth and invited him in.

His tongue met mine, soft, sensual interlacing. The crowd around us seemed to disappear. His arms wrapped around me, closing me into his chest.

It took the music stopping for our hypnotic state to end and bring us back to reality. The band announced it was taking a break and that fireworks would be starting in a few minutes, now that darkness had finally settled in.

Coach and I held hands for the first time and retreated through the crowd, returning to his truck. We decided to watch the fireworks, but wanted to find a better location. We drove a few blocks down on a quiet street. I was practically vibrating in my seat. We found a skate park and tennis court with a small parking lot facing the direction of the festival that was the perfect private viewpoint. Only a few show cars from the festival were parked over here, all empty. The owners had likely decided to take a break and go enjoy some of the sights and sounds themselves.

Coach started to pull into the parking lot; but I couldn't wait any longer. His turn signal was blinking, and he was waiting for a long line of traffic to pass before he could make his turn. I turned in my seat to face him and started unzipping my jean shorts.

"What are you doing?" He asked, casting a sideways look at me, trying not to be distracted from driving.

"Celebrating."

Was my only response as I slipped my hand down inside my shorts, my legs splayed so he could visually treat himself. I began to rub.

Coach's eyes widened, and he couldn't help but stare, feasting his eyes. A car honked behind us, bringing his concentration back to the road, and he made his turn into the parking lot. He kept glancing over at me, watching, as he sought out a spot to pull into. He managed to locate one, but his focus was so compromised he didn't even turn off the truck. He only managed to put it in park, before veering his head back in my direction to once again watch.

I massaged my pearl; exuding confidence. I Wanted him to watch, to visually please him. After all the day's highlights, a physical release would definitely be the cherry on top of my day and his.

I fingered myself, slowly, letting him relish every second. Alternating between rubbing and fingering. Let him see how wet I was getting. I wanted to turn him on, wanted him to see how excited I was for him.

He licked his lips, listening to the sounds of my pleasure, famished with want.

I was plenty warmed up, now to get him ready. I left one hand down my shorts and crawled across the seat and used my right hand to pull at his jeans, locking his gaze again. I unzipped his fly and tugged down his shorts. His massive hard on sprung up. I rubbed myself more, oh how I wanted him!

I clutched his shaft and knelt over him, feeding his cock down my throat. Smelling his pheromones embedded in his intoxicating scent.

I slid my lips up and down his pole, tasting him. I let him feel the walls of my throat close around him before pulling him back up into my mouth and bathing him in my saliva once again. With each plunge down he'd release a deep throaty growl. His dick would stiffen. I wasn't sure how it could get any harder, but I swore it did.

I continued to finger and rub, longing for it to be his meat pushing into me, knowing the anticipation would make it all that much more enjoyable when the time came. He reached around my back end, and I felt him tracing the hem of my shorts, trying to find an opening. It didn't take him long to locate, and one of his big fingers prodded, his hand cupping my ass cheek. He squeezed when his finger came up coated in my lady dew, pleased to feel I was primed. I pulled my hand up to just work my clit, allowing him to slide his finger up and in. He moaned as he dipped it inside me while I simultaneously sunk his meat down my gullet again; foreshadowing what was to come. He pushed in, making every attempt to get in as deep as he could before pulling back out, circling my vulva then slowly pushing in again. A rhythmic and sensual warmup.

I deep throated his hog again and again, curled my tongue up and down his rock hard prick, sucking his knob like it was a cherry tootsie pop. I lapped the salty trickle emitting from his crown. Tasted him and used it like lip gloss to slide my lips back down him, sinking down his rod and licking his balls. I gagged a little as his dick went past the point my reflex could handle. He hissed with pleasure as my throat closed in on him.

My clit was ripe and I was broken in for entry. I lifted my head to take off my shirt and mount him. My shirt was halfway over my head when I heard the door of the truck open. I quickly threw my shirt aside and looked over to see what the heck was going on. He had slid himself out and was beckoning to me.

This could be fun, I thought, as I followed him out. The sound of the last band was carrying through the air, echoing off the city buildings and reverberating back at us. Coach had walked behind the truck, folded down the tailgate, and I pursued, my curiosity piquing. I was still topless, with just my bra and ripped jean shorts on. Any normal day, I would have felt exposed and vulnerable, but not tonight. I was too turned on. I just wanted to get back to business. Getting within his radius, he grabbed me from behind, drawing me into his embrace. His pants he'd tugged down fully exposing his manhood and just hanging off his ass. His lips began kissing the back and sides of my neck, sweeping the loose strands of my hair out of the way. I could feel his veiny erection pushing into my backside, and I pushed back into him. His right hand sank down and guided his cock up the hem of my shorts and lined up at my entrance. He pushed in and I gasped, not having experienced the magnitude of his dick from this position before. He groped my tits, thrusting his meat up inside me . I cranked my head back to the night sky in ecstasy as he continued kissing and fucking me.

The firework show started suddenly with a *crack!* Explosion after explosion lit up the sky, illuminating our x-rated activities for the world to see, had any spectators been around. I found it arousing, to know at any second a passerby may potentially see us. The bass of the music seemed in sync with the crack of each firework as they shot up. Coach's movements began to sync up with it as well, with each explosion he'd do a big thrust in, hitting my cervix wall. I reached over my head behind me, stroking his head and neck, wanting to reciprocate in any way I could. More so than just letting him fuck me over his tailgate.

My shorts were wet with my arousal, each push in, I could feel a gush squirt out and around his shaft, lubing him for the next plunge in. He tugged my bra down from the front, exposing my breasts, then massaged them more. I felt them bounce as he drilled me. I ground my ass into him, wanted to make sure there wasn't a centimeter of length not inside me; I wanted it all.

"Get up on the tailgate." I commanded.

I could tell he was wondering why on Earth I'd change our rhythm right at that moment when he was ready to get off, but he didn't argue. He did what he was told.

He pulled out and quickly hopped up on the tailgate with his legs hanging. I let my shorts fall to the ground and crawled on top of him, reverse cowgirl. Sliding his girth back up inside me, I leaned forward, using my abs for leverage, and clung to the ridge of the tailgate and ground my hips into his crotch. With each eruption from above, I'm sure he could see all the action, and that's what I wanted for him. A visual feast to heighten his erotic experience and fuel his imagination for solo intimate acts for weeks to come.

My legs splayed around him, lips parted around his cock, seeing his manhood sliding in and out of me. My wetness surrounded him, welcoming him in. My backside reared up toward his face and then forward again. He grabbed my hips and began ramming himself into me as I ground down on him.

The cheers from the crowd echoed across the plains, and we knew our time was short before the show was over.

His heaves came in quicker succession. His cock swelled up, filling me even more. There was no vacant space to be had. The added bulk pressed into my g-spot, amping me for a climactic ending. We both humped wildly, and the tailgate shook with our ecstatic motions.

The grand finale of fireworks lit up the night sky, each spark illuminating the night sky one after another in rapid great succession. I felt the powerful surge of fluid rush up his cock and flood inside me with one last huge thrust. My pussy clamped around him and I let go as well, feeling my walls enclose on him, sealing him inside me. The fireworks weren't just in the sky now, but embedded behind my eyelids. Sparks shot every which way, blinding me. I felt the energy and ecstasy as I came surge up through my cervix, my clit, my entire body.

We were both left breathless and perspiring. Neither of us wanted to move, but time was of the essence as we could hear the herds of people flooding down the streets, returning to their vehicles. I reluctantly slid forwards, swept my legs out from behind him and forward in order for me to land on them as I jumped onto the pavement. I snatched my damp shorts off the ground and re-dressed. I stuffed my tits back in my bra and opened the truck to grab my shirt. Coach was reapplying his clothes as well before opening his truck's rear cab door.

He had a cooler in the backseat. He reefed it out, producing two glass necked beer bottles. Icy cold even.

"What's all this?"

I asked half laughing at the spontaneity of him having cold beers in his truck ready to drink.

"Can never be too prepared." He said with a wink. He hopped back onto the tailgate, patting the seat next to him, inviting me to join him. He handed me a bottle and we cracked them open.

"You know, I don't even know your name." I whispered to him as I leaned against his side.

I could hear him let out a breath, as if bracing himself for a blow to the gut.

"It's Austin," he said eventually.

I took a long sip, savoring its taste, and propped my head on his shoulder.

"I like it...Austin." I replied.

I took another long sip as we stared off into the cascading darkness and watched the unknowing crowd of vehicles disperse into the night.

14

Coach

Word of the team's success traveled like wildfire around the area. They even made the local news, as well as the front page of the newspaper. My gym's popularity skyrocketed even more following the publicity, and I ended up having to hire a receptionist and source out some of my adult students to be teachers and teaching assistants just to handle the immense workload we acquired.

Josh was one for my Kamloops gym, and I made Cooper one of my assistants at the Sorrento gym. I wanted to be able to pay him a wage, and give him a headstart. Possibly even take some of the pressure off his mom and reward him for his hard work and dedication. He took right to it and was great with the kids.

New faces were always popping up at the gym. It was getting hard for me to keep track of everyone. One face however, really popped out to me. He was an older man, I'd say his early sixties. Close to my height, a scraggly beard, dark gray furrowed eyes. He looked so familiar, yet I couldn't place him. He began attending classes spectating at my Sorrento location.

At first I brushed it off thinking he must be a grandparent to one or more of my students, as quite often grandparents would drop off and pick up or stay to observe. But after a few weeks or so, I started seeing red flags. I never saw him leave with any kids, never saw any kids approach him, and yet he was always staring. Whenever I was at the center of the mats teaching, I felt his eyes locked on our group. Had he been an interested patron, I assumed he would have watched a class or two and then approached me to ask questions about enrollment or something of that sort. But it had been weeks, and nothing had come of his interest. I had started to have suspicions about his presence there. I didn't want my gym becoming a breeding ground for child predators. I decided to confront him.

I had been waiting for him to arrive so I could talk to him prior to class starting. However, he didn't arrive with the students, and I was forced to begin class without having a face to face with him.

Approximately twenty minutes into class, I noticed him slip through the door and sneak into the group of parents up top in the viewing section.

I spent the majority of class subtly observing him through my peripherals, making sure he wasn't going to attempt to sneak out as well.

Class ended and the cluster of adults made their way down the stairs. Some b-lined for the door whilst others helped their little ones gather their things or put on their boots and shoes. The *guy* was one of the ones that charged for the door. I cut in front, not wanting to draw attention, but also avoid him taking off. I managed to get ahead of him and stretch my arm casually across his path, barricading him in. He was trapped between the wall and the flock of parents and kids still making their exit. If he were to try to merge into the traffic, he would end up making a scene as he would have to stuff himself into one of their sides to accomplish such a feat.

I definitely startled him when I propped my arm up in front of him. I gave him a wry smile, letting my eyes twinkle at him in a condescending way. Moments passed, and I waited there patiently until the last patron exited the establishment.

"Excuse me, may I go now?"

He asked me in a gruff annoyed tone.

"Actually mate, I wanted to have a few words with you, if you'd be so kind." I made it sound like he had an option, but I think he noted that he didn't have an option at all. I steered him towards my desk, putting myself between him and the door before I began in on him.

"I've noticed you've been attending for quite a few weeks now. Can you tell me who you're accompanying?"

The man looked at me scornfully, knowing he couldn't just make up any old name, or I'd for sure know he was lying.

"I'm not accompanying anyone."

"Ok, well can you tell me your name and reasoning for attending a kids martial arts class?"

I stared at him up and down, making a full description in my brain in case I was forced to call the cops to report him.

"My name isn't any of your business, and I just happen to enjoy martial arts."

He sneered at me.

"Well, unfortunately for you, you're going to have to keep your love for martial arts at home on the television from now on. I don't condone random people off the street coming into my gym watching kids."

I was firm, leaving no room for my words to be misconstrued.

"You think I'm here to watch the *kids*?"

A look of disgust and disbelief crossed his face. My subtle accusation must have hit a nerve.

"Not sure who else you'd be watching." I shrugged. It was the truth.

"Wow. Ok then, I can see this isn't going in the direction I hoped it would."

He started to walk around me towards the door. I considered my words heeded and allowed him to exit, his words thought-provoking.

What did he mean? The direction he hoped it would? Did he mean for us to have this conversation one day? Who was this man?

I didn't have long to ponder, as the teen class rolled in. My fifteen minute break had ended.

15

Weeks flew by, and Paige and my relationship continued to grow, although we still kept it behind closed doors. I appreciated her discretion. I knew she was a private person as well, and the more I could keep people's noses out of my private matters the better, for her and for me. I didn't want anyone digging around in my past, marring the new name I had made for myself and my reputation. I could only imagine what turmoil would become of things if the likes of Becky Carlyle found out I had a love interest.

Love... I hadn't even said it before. The thought had just never crossed my mind, until Paige. Now here I had referenced my relationship with her as my love interest. A smile crossed my lips. The emptiness I'd always felt had nearly disappeared in the last few months, now that Paige was a part of my life.

My mother sensed the improvement in mood in our phone calls and had finally questioned me about it. I didn't hesitate to tell her. I didn't keep secrets from my mother. I was eager to tell her I thought I'd found someone that made me happy, shared my interests. She was elated for me and had me describe her. She agreed Paige sounded like a good match for me. It felt good to finally tell someone and share my happiness.

Everyday with Paige was magical, every aspect- eating, hanging out, sparring, fishing, 4x4ing, dancing, cuddling, and especially love-making. I was pretty certain she felt as strongly as I did. I may have been a few years her senior, but she was so in tune with all my thoughts and interests, we paid it no heed. I longed to be able to hold her hand out in public though, let the world know she was mine. I was not oblivious to the fact that she was a gorgeous woman and stole the attention of many men as she went about her days. I'd never had any reason to feel jealous before, but I definitely felt a twinge of it every time I'd see a guy walk by and turn to do a double take at her ass. It happened a lot too. She paid it no mind. I don't know if she just didn't notice or couldn't be bothered. I admired her unfaltering loyalty.

I hated to admit that Cooper's mother, another woman, had inspired me to renovate the small room under the stairs, but that is definitely where the idea came from. As Paige and I were spending more and more time together, bouncing between locations, I wanted something fun for us when sporadic moments like we had shared previously in the Kamloops gym came about.

I painted the walls a deep indigo blue and added a small candelabra chandelier. It filled the small space with its warm glow. White baseboards and trim brightened the room a bit. I installed a Deluxe Fetish Sex Swing and decided if I was going to go that far, I might as well purchase a few other fun accessories. I loaded up with a strict leather scottish tawse, a restraint kit with various leather straps and gags, a set of four Magnus ultra powerful magnetic orbs, anal beads, and a steel ball head ring and a few other impulsive purchases.

I hung a handful of hooks in order to organize my loot so that it was out of the way, but in such a manner I could tantalize her. See what drew her focus and desire. So there they dangled, awaiting their moment. A small ornate shelf held a series of lubricants, all with different tasks; numbing, warming, flavored, clit stimulating, etcetera.

I never imagined I'd be able to fit it all in the room, but after removing the cleaning supplies and boxes that had occupied the space beforehand, I found the room actually had a fair bit of space. I looked around at the completed chamber and hoped Paige would be open to exploring different venues of pleasure.

I couldn't wait to surprise her with it. I had added a deadbolt to the door with a keypad lock. That way I could guarantee no one but myself and Paige would know what was behind our closed doors.

My Wild Dogs team had upped their training the past few weeks as well. We had entered every tournament we could and came home with gold more often than not. Paige had yet to lose a match. The more experience they had, the faster paced their fights became. Their timing and execution of techniques were now damned near flawless.

Cooper was making enough working for me that he was able to afford his competition fees and fight in the tournaments now as well. I noticed he looked better fed, his face fuller and his muscles able to grow with the added weight he now had. He seemed like a new kid; happy and fulfilled.

Connie was looking happier and healthier as well. There was a serene calmness about her. Less stressed with making enough money now at her new job. She had a new found confidence and no longer skulked away from the crowd of ladies watching their little ones. She partook in their conversations, and her face beamed when she'd smile at their jokes. The dark circles around her eyes had finally faded away. She kept her distance from me though, and I from her. There was no animosity between us. I think she knew what had been at stake before and caught on that discretion was key. I was happy to see that her and Cooper's lives were improving.

I was still on edge having Paige attend the Sorrento gym though. Becky Carlyle still hovered at every class at both locations. I hated the idea that she might connect the dots, seeing Paige now attending the Sorrento gym as well as the Kamloops one. I feared Becky would spitefully reveal our previous arrangement to Paige. I knew, even though it had occurred prior to me even meeting Paige, that those actions would cause her pain. Hell, they caused me nausea even still.

Every class, I could feel Becky's eyes boring into my backside. She'd attempt to steal my focus, making subtle sexual motions with her mouth and hands so that only I could see them. I avoided eye contact as much as possible, trying to focus on my classes.

She couldn't possibly think I'd ever be interested in participating in such acts with her ever again, could she? I grimaced at the very thought. Paige was the only one I wanted to be with now. My thoughts and eyes hadn't strayed ever since we first connected. I wanted her and her alone, and I wasn't about to let anything or anyone jeopardize that. Even my history with the likes of Becky Carlyle.

I wasn't sure how I was going to safeguard my awful truth, but I knew I needed to in order to sustain the relationship.

15.5
Paige

I had won my last five fights. When I wasn't training, working or competing, you could find me with Austin. He still preferred me to call him Coach. But in my mind, I was calling him by his given name. We'd grown so close that whenever I was able, I had started spending nights at his place in Sorrento and attending the Sorrento gym.

Austin seemed to enjoy my company during the nights. However, he always seemed nervous when I was at the gym there. I could have been misreading things, but that was just how it felt at the time. When we were one on one training there it was fine. He only seemed off when there were crowds, parents and kids alike, hovering or watching.

He started spending nights at my place in Kamloops as well. It saved him multiple trips throughout the week, or a few later nights at the very least.

Those were my favorite nights. Getting to spend time with Austin; one on one, in his arms and him in between my legs. We'd cook together, eat, shower, sleep, and every other activity in between. It was exactly the circumstances I always imagined I'd find myself in with a partner. Everything was perfect.

That was until I started to get the lingering feeling I was being watched. I couldn't shake the feeling. It always seemed to come about at the gym. Didn't seem to matter which gym. I would scan my surroundings, looking for the source of the looming feeling. I could never pinpoint it. I chalked it up to me being paranoid, but for what reason I wasn't sure. I'd never been paranoid before. Perhaps I was feeding off Coach's vibes. His worry of judgment surrounding our relationship, and now I was constantly on watch in order to protect his reputation. Yes, that must be it.

Satisfied with my conclusion, I tried to push it from my mind and ignore when the thoughts crept up on me. However, despite my many efforts, I still couldn't shake the feeling...

16

Coach

I covered her eyes. I wanted to surprise her with it. Classes were done for the day, and she thought we'd just be doing our normal routine. I had other plans.

She was giggling as I guided her over to the doorway, ready to unveil. One...Two... On three I pulled my hands away. She blinked, staring at the white door, looking around thinking she was missing something. I didn't make any attempt to hide my amusement, and she turned to smack me.

"You got me all excited for nothing. Pretending there was a surprise for me. You're a jerk." She was laughing, and I chuckled along with her as I reached forward and punched in the code on the electric security system. Her laughter ceased, and she looked back at the door, realizing she hadn't noticed the lock. I reached inside the door frame, flicked on the light, and stepped aside, swinging the door open as I did. Allowing her the first viewing of the completed room.

She stepped forward, her eyes wide. I couldn't read her expression. *Was she in shock? Did she like it? Was she curious at all? Or perhaps she realized I might be a bit too extreme for her and was having regrets getting involved with me?*

The indigo blue walls glowed in the soft yellow lighting. The many toys I had filled the space with were all on display, ready and waiting. The swing suspended from the ceiling, hanging; anticipating.

"What is this?"

She asked inquisitively, clearly dumbfounded as her voice wavered in uncertainty.

"I know it seems like a lot. If you're not into it, that's fine. I just wanted to create a space, just for us. I've always had...urges. I was hoping maybe you'd be willing to explore them with me?" I didn't pause long enough to leave her time to answer. I carried on.

"If you don't want to, it's ok, I still want to be with you. I just was giving it a shot. Why not, right?"

Her gaze floated back and forth between me and the room. Her silence seemed to be the response I was dreading. She didn't even know how to react. I had mortified her.

"Listen, forget I even brought it up. I'll take it all down."

I hung my head embarrassed and turned to walk away, swinging the door closed as I exited to the gym. She followed me out, and we went about the remainder of our day in silence.

So kink was a breaking point for her, I noted. From now on, I'd be sure to push down all of my deepest desires. I was disappointed, but I knew I'd rather have a life with Paige than none. If it meant hanging up some of my compulsions, well so be it.

The awkward silence that hovered throughout that day was the worst. I wished I could have gone back in time and dismissed the notion that she may have been into any of my undisclosed sexual interests prior to creating that silly room. I hated that her disinterest made me ponder our relationship altogether. I was happy now, that I couldn't deny, but if she didn't share the same interests or passions, perhaps that meant we wouldn't be as compatible as I'd once thought.

I avoided prolonged eye contact. The small amount of conversation we shared was short, curt responses. I wasn't sure how to talk about it, hoped she'd just eventually forget about it. But that was wishful thinking.

She excused herself that evening, said she had things she needed to get done in Kamloops. It was hard not to look into it further. Scenarios kept running through my mind, all negative. I figured; *so this is how it ends?*

A knot formed in my gut.

I bid her farewell, we exchanged emotionless pecks on the cheek, and she slipped away. I choked down my feelings and instead turned to my beer fridge for consolation. It was a good thing my fridge had been fairly well stocked, as one after another, each bottle of amber liquid disappeared with increased ease and speed.

I kicked the two empty beer boxes to the side as I made my way back to the house, teetering as I walked. I released an enormous belch, fumigating my entryway as I kicked off my shoes, stumbling up the steps to the kitchen then down the hall to my room. I didn't even bother changing. I flopped on the bed, and that's where my memory went blank.

I woke with a start. My head was pounding. Sitting up, I sat for a moment attempting to open my eyes when a sudden surge of vomit fueled me to sprint to the ensuite. I collapsed into my toilet bowl, evacuating my stomach contents with a series of tremendous gut lurches and heaves. Breathing heavy, I reached over and grabbed a towel to wipe the remaining contents and stringy spittle off my lips. My skin was clammy and hot. I rested my forehead on my arm, leaning on the bowl's edge.

I focused my attention on the floor in hopes if I were to focus elsewhere, the pounding in my head would eventually just disappear. Instead, I noticed something I hadn't before. I was wearing my shoes, and a thick layer of mud was half dried to the soles. As I lifted my head in order to survey, I observed clumps of the mud had fallen off in a trail on my way to the bathroom.

I swore I removed my shoes prior to going to bed last night. I also didn't recall walking through mud. I must have just been too drunk and couldn't recall correctly was what I summed it up to.

Brushing it from my thoughts, I heaved myself up and retraced my muddy footprints through the house and back to the entrance. I removed my shoes and clapped them together out the door, knocking the remaining dirt off, before grabbing the broom to sweep up the mess. I found a handful of crumpled cash and a small wad of paper with a pen scratched phone number on it that was barely readable on my kitchen counter. I didn't remember emptying my pockets the night before either. Nor did I remember where I would have gotten the phone number. It did not appear to be my writing, unless in my inebriated state I possibly wrote differently. I couldn't rule that out. *But whose number was it, and why would I have written it down?*

Dismissing my paranoid thoughts, I decided a shower was in order and yanked my shirt off as I strode in the direction of the bathroom.

I turned the taps on and removed my remaining clothing. Upon removing my boxer briefs, I became aware that something was on me. I looked down. A condom hung from the tip of my flaccid dick.

My breath caught in my throat, and I looked up to catch sight of my reflection in the mirror. My face was pale and chalky as the color drained from it. There's only one implication I could connect with the evidence at hand...

Snatching my towel and wrapping it around my waist I bolted to the gym. The secret room's door laid ajar, the lights still aglow. Various toys laid on the floor, clearly used.

I felt a surge of disgust bubble up like acid being poured on my heart. *Who on Earth did I have in this room with me last night?* I was not fool enough to think Paige had come back that same evening to test it out. Repulsed, I yanked the condom off my cock and threw it in the trash bin, cursing myself. I was a complete fuck up.

16.5

Paige

He had revealed the room to me early that day. I was more than shocked. I couldn't find words. Throughout the day I felt the weight of that silence. I had never felt uncomfortable with Coach ever before this, but now...I wasn't sure what to think, what to make of it. Deep down, I knew he was likely pretty kinky. I just wasn't aware the extent of it. *Was I ready for that?* It likely wasn't too far of a jump from our already libidinous relationship, but in my mind it seemed leaps and bounds away.

I needed time to think. Some space away from his scrutinous eyes. Feeling him examining me from a distance all day, full well knowing he was awaiting a response from me, it was pressure I didn't want to deal with at that very moment. I wanted to mull it over, weigh my options and make a decision based on what I felt was best. I didn't need Coach's influence possibly making an impression on my decision. I decided to head home that evening so I could have the time to think.

Coach didn't seem pleased when I told him I was leaving. His kiss was cold and calculated, no emotion. But alas, I'm sure mine was also lacking its usual vigor as my brain was going a mile a minute. We opted for kisses on the cheeks instead of the mouth. Also a clear indication we weren't completely present in the moment. I had hoped Coach wouldn't read into it, I was just contemplating.

That night I researched. Watched testimonials and documentaries. Anything I could think of to make sure I was fully informed. Then as I was lying in bed, I let my emotions finally enter the equation. *Did I love this man? Would I do anything for him?* And most of all...*Did I trust him?*

A few days passed. I focused on work and my training. Coach was still very quiet and introverted. I had no opportunity yet to discuss my decision with him and wasn't sure how to open up that conversation. I figured I'd wait until the perfect moment arose. It was difficult to determine when that moment would be though.

Coach seemed so distant, not his usual self. He seemed to be avoiding me. Even in our private lessons he was all business. He hadn't asked if I'd be coming to the Sorrento gym and spending the night like I usually would. I decided maybe I would just show up and see what would happen. *Maybe he just needed some time as well?*

I arrived a bit earlier than I normally would have. I guess I just wanted to see him in his element, perhaps have a bit more time to think of a conversation starter. As I was approaching the gym, an older gentleman was hovering around one of the windows. He puffed on a cigarette as he viewed the class through the clear pane, blowing long billowing smoke clouds into the brisk air. His eyes were brooding and set. He barely noticed me as I approached. I must have startled him, as he jumped slightly and shuffled away from the window. I assumed he was either a parent or grandparent to one of Coach's students.

"Don't mind me. You can keep watching, I'll just slip in."

"Thank you." He said offhanded, seeming a bit unsure.

"You're Paige Bryant aren't you?"

"Yes, that's me. I train here occasionally as well as in Kamloops."

"You're a great fighter. And you look so familiar, just can't peg where I recognize you from."

"Well thank you, that's very kind. I can't take all the credit though, I have a great coach. And yeah, not sure where you'd know me from, sorry." We exchanged smiles, his a little more subdued as he took another long drag of his smoke. I did have to admit, there was something very familiar about this man. Perhaps I had just seen him on the sidelines of coach's classes before.

"Have a great day!" I waved as I entered the building. He nodded his goodbye and ashed his cigarette with his toe.

I crept into the building, trying not to disturb the ongoing class. However, upon entering, I instantly felt Coach's eyes look my way. He was busy wrapping up the class with a last minute speech. I opted to ignore his gaze and snuck into the changeroom to get ready for my session. As I changed, I could hear the commotion as students and guardians alike exited the building. I stepped out and found Coach solo, cleaning the mats quickly prior to our session.

I approached him gingerly, walking up whilst his back was still turned to me.

"Hey, I've been meaning to talk to you," I trailed on. He didn't bother to turn to face me. *Maybe he's still pissed?*

"Oh yeah? Whatever about?" he responded very nonchalantly.

"Well, about the other night...the room. I just needed time to think."

"Think? You left. I assumed that was your response. I got over it, it's fine."

"Yeah, I needed time, some space to think. Wait, what do you mean you *got over it?*"

My nerves suddenly all stood on end. His voice was so full of malice. I didn't assume he was being this cold coincidentally.

"I'm over it. That's all I have to say. Now are you wanting to train or not?"

This was not him. This was not MY Austin. Something was up. Pushing my exasperation to his comments aside, I made a bold move, wanting to reclaim what was mine. Make him see my heart.

I took his gi by the collar and reefed him to his feet, spinning him around to face me. I peered up into his eyes, examining him closely. His gray eyes clouded. I could tell he was emotional, hence his attitude. I must have hurt him. He'd never admit it, he was too proud. But I could see right through him. I drug him over to the room.

"Punch in the damn code." I demanded.

"What for?"

"Just do it."

Reluctantly, he pushed in each button, I felt my heart pound as I realized it was a date. The date we consummated our relationship.

He opened the door and flicked on the dim lighting. That was my chance. I shoved his back against the doorframe and smooshed my lips on his. I wrapped my arms around his neck, forcing him to kiss me back. He wasn't getting away that easy.

I could feel him hesitating. I had taken him by surprise. I squeezed him tighter, pressing my body into his, letting him know it was ok. Finally his arms wrapped themselves around my waist. His fingers gripped my back, digging in, clinging to me, not wanting me to slip through his fingers again. We kissed passionately, enveloping each other in our yearning. I wanted nothing more than to be with this man, no matter what that entailed.

I peeled off my sports bra, exposing my breasts to him. His eyes lingered on them before his gaze rose to meet mine and locked there. I ripped his belt and gi top off and threw them across the gym, all the while pulling him into the room with me, sealing the door behind us.

17

Coach

It felt so good to be in her arms again though. Feeling her body against mine. Smelling her intoxicating scent. I felt vulnerable. I couldn't tell her. I couldn't break her heart like that. The truth would die with me. Or at least I could stall telling her until the right time. Either way, I couldn't tell her at that moment, as dishonorable as I knew it was.

I couldn't lose her.

I let myself be consumed by her, felt the passion flare between us as she pulled me into that little room and closed the door behind us. She was giving herself to me completely. I couldn't refuse her. I wanted her, and only her.

Her bare breasts caused me to stiffen instantly. *Boy I was a lucky man.* I fumbled with her pant strings until they finally fell to the floor. Her black laced panties against her gorgeous bronzed skin was enough to drive any fella crazy. I seized her ass, felt her plump muscular cheeks fill my palms. My erection was full mast, tenting out my pants. Her hands groped my body, working their way down before clutching my manhood. Her hands worked fast, yanking the last of my clothes off. She was ready to kneel, but I had other ideas.

I ripped her panties from her body, lifted her into the air and walked her back into the eagerly awaiting swing that hung in the corner, sticking her ass and legs into its stirrups. She gawked at me with those beautiful doe eyes of hers, nervous and innocent.

"It's okay, relax." I relayed calmly.

"I'd never do anything you weren't comfortable with. We can make a safe word." She nodded that she was agreeable to that.

"Ok, how about...cinnamon?" A faint smile crossed her lips and she nodded again. It was an easy one. I didn't want to be a jerk and give her something difficult like worcestershire just to be mean. I wanted her first experience to be enjoyable. I wanted her to want to do it all again, explore more with me. That would mean baby steps, sticking within her comfort zone for the first bit until she eventually grew a taste for it. I hoped she would.

My eyes scoped my various accumulation of toys. Searching for which would be the chosen one for our first erotic rendezvous to christen the room.

As soon as I saw them, I knew.

She was attempting to peer over my shoulder, curious which item I would pick. I turned back to her, and she looked at me questioningly. She couldn't see what I had picked. Walking forward, I held out my closed fists to her.

"Pick a hand, any hand."

She bit her lip and lifted an eyebrow to me, surveying both my fists before pointing at my left.

"You're sure?" She nodded again and continued to watch my hands to see what was in each of them. I opened my palms and revealed the four magnetic orbs. They looked harmless enough, just four shiny silver balls in my hand. I could tell she didn't know what to think of this surprise. She had no idea what pleasure these little balls could bring.

I tilted her back in her swing. Using some of the leather restraints in my collection, I tethered her wrists and ankles to the straps of the swing. Then taking just two of the orbs, I placed one on either side of her right nipple and let go. She jumped the instant I released them. The magnetic force of the balls suctioned them together, compressing her nipple.

"Breathe." I told her.

A rattled breath escaped her teeth. They could hurt. I knew this, and it was a pain she hadn't been made aware of before, especially in such a sensitive area.

“Now the next.” I motioned to her other breast, and she sucked in some wind, nodding again. Prying the balls apart, I once again placed them on either side of her taffy nipple before releasing them. She jumped again.

I stepped back slightly to admire her. Her tan skin sitting amidst the leather swing straps, legs spread, and the two silver orbs clamping her nipples tight. It appeared as if she had her nipples pierced, which I had to admit was kind of hot. I loved her boobs just how they were, but they could definitely pull off some piercings if she ever wanted to take that leap.

I kneeled down between her legs and pulled her pussy in towards me, like a hearty meal being airlifted down to a gaggle of avalanche survivors that hadn’t eaten for days.

I started slow. Sniffed her snatch, her finely manicured tiny triangle of pubes holding in her delectable aroma. Brown sugar, mmm… My mouth was salivating for her. I licked up her slit, ever so lightly, just to give her a taste of what was to come. Waited a few seconds then ran my tongue up her slit again, this time a little deeper. Waited a few milliseconds more and then repeated again and again. Letting my saliva moisten her lips, allowing her excitement to build with my gradual licks instead of giving it to her all at once. Each time my tongue made contact with her bits, her back would arc, her legs would splay wider, and her muff would push into my face eager for more. It was as if it were inviting me to have another helping, which I did so rapturously.

I dived in, tongue now thrashing her clit and vulva, sucking her puss like a blood thirsty vampire. Listening to her squeals, my cock swelled further, my erection pulsating with the vast amount of blood coursing through it.

It was so hot watching her writhe aimlessly in her swing. A prisoner to whatever course of actions I chose to unleash on her. The orbs remained clamped on her areolas, bedazzling her breasts. They didn’t budge as her body rolled and swayed, squirming in ecstasy. Wanting to heighten her experience, I slipped a digit up inside her so I could simultaneously finger her, all the while feasting on her clam. She released an exulted squeal and began rocking herself into me, pushing my finger in deeper and deeper. I tongued her lady dew off the base of my finger with each pull away, tasting her essence. I wrapped my mouth over her entire surface and sucked her like an oyster from its shell. I couldn't get enough. Swallowing her flavor, I wanted more, needed it.

Her pearl ripe with arousal, her juices sloshing, it sparked me to push more boundaries, be even bolder. I inserted another digit, letting my fingers fill her. Not done yet, I raised my pinky finger, slathering it in the mixture of saliva and lady cum before easing it into her backdoor.

Her body instantly froze, paralyzed as I stun gunned her. I didn't let her shock stop me from continuing my procession of exploration. I prodded away, fingering her front and back, whilst eating her, matching my rhythm to the sway of the swing. She succumbed, hanging there completely in my control. Our secretions dribbled down, keeping my pinky lubricated as I thrust in and out of her. Her body trembled and convulsed. It was about all she could do, that and scream. I reveled in the elation I was providing her, and the feeling of power I had over her body. Reducing her to a quivering puddle of lady cum and whimpers was the ultimate aphrodisiac.

With a few more finger thrusts in I felt the familiar tightening that signaled me she was about to blow. I intensified my licking and sucking, wanting to throw her over the top with euphoria. With one diaphragm bursting wail she let go. A harmoniously erotic holler bounced off the closet walls, filling my ears. Juices squirted, filling my mouth and spraying my face and hand. I swallowed and tried to suck every last drop I could manage, suckling my knuckles thirstily.

She slung there, panting and lifeless. I couldn't help but smile. Clearly I had done well. I eased my digits out of her orifices and stood up. Seeing my lips curled she attempted to kick her foot at me without much success as she was still bound to the swing.

"Shut up you." She said coyly, half laughing and trying to hide her face.

"I didn't say a thing." I winked at her, then bowed down to remove the orbs from her breasts. Reddened dimples were the only tell tale sign that they'd been squeezed excessively only seconds before.

"You were right though...wow! The pain mixed with the pleasure, and then being tied up on top of that. Having to give up that control...it really did it for me, babe." Her expression was earnest.

"I'm just grateful you were willing to give it a chance. But... we're not done yet." She gawked at me, stunned.

"There's more?"

"I didn't make an entire secret room with just two toys in it. Of course there's more."

"I just want your dick!" She said it in such a way, I felt myself jolt with excitement.

"Well...I believe I can squeeze that in. No pun intended." I winked at her again and she stifled a laugh.

I reached over and toweled off my hand before returning to my assortment of toys. I knew exactly which one was next to try. I picked out a little silver balled contraption. Knowing full well she'd never guess what it was or its use. I turned to face her and she studied it, trying to decipher. I lowered it, slipping it over the crown of my cock. The ball hovered on the lower end of my glans, right where I'd really feel its presence. It resembled a chastity cage but left the head exposed. I could already feel the pressure of the ball pushing into me.

"What's that for?"

"Oh, you'll see."

I positioned myself between her legs, it was my turn now.

She remained perfectly soaking wet. Her pussy still tightened after her massive orgasm. I shoved my dick in as deep as I could. Her warm wet walls closed in around me, squeezing me tight. It was pure ecstasy.

I began thrusting my hips in, finding that familiar clefted pleasure point and focused my dick's tip there. Her head lulled back.

"Oh my god! Oh my fucking god! What is that thing? That feels ah-ah-Amazing!" She could barely utter the words out. The ball head ring was doing its job for both of us. I grunted my satisfaction feeling its pressure weighted on my own sweet spot. Heightening the sensation and adding just enough added friction, it ascended my climax to a new elevation.

Her clit was already engorged and hypersensitive from her first orgasm, so I knew the second wouldn't be far off. With a few quick pulls, I managed to untie the straps that held her in place and flipped her over in the swing, ass up and out. With no hesitation at all, I stuffed my cock back inside and pounded her hard, plunging my meat in relentlessly. Her tits protruded through the bottom of the swing, as her top half was shoved into its depths.

My dick was rock hard pummeling into her well lubricated crevice with her ass hovering in the air. I grasped her thick thighs and used them as anchors to pull her into me. I throttled on, shoving my hog as deep in as I could get. Hitting the wall of her cervix with each almighty heave.

Her shrieks alerted me that she was on the cusp. I was kegel locked and had to ram my cock in even harder to continue to hit that delightful zone again and again. I felt that oh so familiar knot, rising through my shaft. The orgasmic build up was even more intense with that little steel ball and ring securely clamped around my manhood. Paige gave a tremendous jolt, her climax finally peaking, and her throaty moans consumed me.

That was it for me. As soon as I heard her orgasming again, I couldn't restrain myself. I released that knot in a chaotic eruption of nectarous oozing semen. I had attempted to pull out, but ended up leaving a trail of sauce seeping out of her like a perfectly cooked hot pocket.

17.5
Paige

Wow! Laying in bed that night I was absolutely still floored from the erotic endeavors of the day. I had never been big into toys. I always thought a good dick was enough. That afternoon changed my whole perspective on things. I felt up under my shirt, massaging my breasts where the orbs had been, kneading the tender areas. It was so odd for me to think that pleasure could come from pain. Yet there I was... still reveling in my sexual elation hours later.

Coach was snoring softly, his warm body radiating heat on me. It was pouring rain outside, and the occasional bolt of lightning lit up the night. I reached over to rub his back, wanting to feel his skin. He had fallen asleep with the bedside lamps still on, and I hadn't yet mustered the energy to get up in order to turn them off. It had been a long day. I knew I needed sleep. I wished Coach had realized he was drifting off and had done me the favor of turning his lamp off at the very least.

I began pulling back my covers in order to get up when I heard some faint scuffling noises. It sounded like something heavy being drug and then a thud. Or could I have been imagining it? The night often played games with people's ears and senses. Walking around the bed, I clicked off the lights and listened for a few seconds longer...nothing but silence. I shrugged, brushed it off as nothing and opted to go to the bathroom before returning to bed.

Upon finishing and exiting the ensuite, another bolt of lightning flashed, casting its brightness through the window. That's when I saw it!

I screamed in surprise, and Coach launched up from his sleep panic stricken.

"What's wrong?"

"There was a face in the window! It was watching me!"

Coach bolted for his gun safe and wrenched it open after punching in his code. His hand reached for his gun and a box of ammo, and he began loading it as he made his way to the front door. I wasn't sure what to do. I felt too disturbed to stay in the room alone, so I followed him.

"Stay inside." He ordered me.

I didn't like the idea of him going out alone, even if I knew he was more than capable of handling himself, but I didn't dare disobey him. Every student of his knew the golden rule: Always obey Coach. That meant don't question him, don't argue with him, just do what you're told.

"Lock the door." He demanded as he stepped out the door and shut it tight behind him.

Turning the deadbolt, I rushed to the back patio door to make sure it was also sealed. As long as I had been staying at the house, that door had always been locked unless we happened to be on the porch or barbecuing, so I wasn't really worried about it. That was until I saw it. The dead bolt wasn't locked. The door hung there slightly ajar, as beads of rainwater dripped onto the living room's vinyl plank flooring .

Immediately perturbed, I fled back to the front door to warn Coach. A sinking feeling settled in my gut, I tore open the door and ran out into the rain.

"Coach! Coach!" I called, casting my eyes this way and that.

I attempted to shield my eyes from the cascading rain drops that were pelting my eyes causing my vision to blur. I ran around the side of the house, my bare feet splashing through the mud and the accumulation of puddles. I was studying the ground, trying to decipher if there were fresh footprints in the turf that may lead me to him. However, the vast amount of water pouring from the sky was quick to wash away any trace he may have left.

Thunder clapped, drowning out my continued hollers. I circled the house, desperate to find him. *Where could he be?* I faintly made out the sound of a muffled shout followed by an onset of trampling steps that grew louder as they approached. Another thunderclap boomed, muting their advance. Without the lightning to set the lawn aglow, I was cast in darkness. Just the shadows offered me mere traces of orientation as I proceeded in the direction I heard the noises coming from. Rocks and twigs jabbed the soles of my feet painfully, but I paid it no heed, not wanting to waste a single second if Coach were to need my help.

I had entered the trees surrounding the outskirts of the property. Branches and brambles smacked my body and face as I charged through, following blindly.

With an almighty *thwack!* The wind was knocked from me, and I was catapulted to the ground. I groaned and heard the frantic scuffling of the individual who had run into me so forcefully before leaping up and running off into the blackness. The whole ordeal was only a fleeting matter of seconds

Another flash of lightning and I could make out footsteps fast approaching. It was Coach. He kneeled down.

"Paige! Are you ok?"

"Yeah, I'm fine. Just winded is all. But..."

"I have him on the run. Get yourself back to the house."

"No, wait! He was in the house, babe. The patio door was open!" Coach stared at me in disbelief, realizing this wasn't likely some random burglar or creep.

"Son of a bitch..." He jolted into a sprint in order to catch up to the intruder, leaving me to pick myself up and trudge back to the house in order to call the cops.

I fumbled aimlessly back through the trees until they began to thin out, and I could tell I was getting closer to the cleared portion near the house.

By the time I reached the house's perimeter, I was shaking with cold and soaked to the bone. I had fled the house with nothing more than a thin fabric t-shirt and pajama shorts on. My cheek had begun to throb. Apparently when the intruder barreled into me he had managed to deck me in the face. My knee and elbow were also scraped up pretty badly on the side that hit the ground. I'm sure I looked in a real fine state.

Ambling to the entranceway, I was a bit leery of reentering the house. An unsettled feeling lingered in the pit of my gut, knowing I had been watched. My privacy had been compromised. Heck, it had been full on invaded. And who knows how long this had been going on for? We could never really know.

Disregarding my concerns for the moment, I pushed forth into the house and called the local precinct. Coach's list of emergency numbers on the fridge that I had always laughed at finally served a valid purpose. At that moment, I was very thankful he had it.

Approximately twenty minutes passed. All I could hear was the clock's ticking, counting down every second that Coach had not returned. When the sirens finally became audible I bounded for the door, running right out to inform them he still wasn't back. I'm sure they could see the worry etched in my face, my body still soaked and chilled. I had been so preoccupied fretting about Coach's whereabouts and his safety. I had completely forgotten about the fact that I was frozen.

The female cop wrapped a wool blanket, retrieved from under her seat, around my shoulders. Its warmth was a meager comfort and mildly eased my uncontrollable shaking. I wasn't even sure if I was shaking from being cold anymore, or if it was due to the substantial amount of anxiety I was having. *Where on Earth could he be? What was taking him so long? Was he ok?* Were all questions floating through my mind again and again.

I relayed my sequence of events to the cop, Officer Davis, as her name tag read. She recorded it all in her little notepad and walked around viewing the entry points as well as the window that I first saw the perpetrator in. Her partner had left with a spotlight to scope out the area and see if he could locate either Coach or the perp.

"Can you describe him to me? The man you saw?"

"I wish I could. I just saw his eyes, not even their color, but more just the whites of them, it was so dark."

"Any details at all, whatever you can remember." I thought hard, trying to recall anything. I shut my eyes and relied on my senses.

"When he knocked into me, out in the woods. He smelt like cigarettes... That's really about the only thing I noticed. That, and he had quite a lot of arm hair. I only noticed because his arm touched mine."

"Okay, well that's a good start. If you think of anything else you can give me a call." She handed me her card with her phone number on it and precinct emblem. I nodded. I had begun biting my nails. Her partner had also not returned yet.

Officer Davis, must have come to the realization she should have heard something from him by now as well and began radioing him for an update.

"You see anything?" *blip*

A few moments of silence.

"Officer Canatelli, do you read me?" *blip*

More silence. The white noise was deafening. I could feel my heart pounding, and caught myself holding my breath. Then...

"Yeah I'm here. I found them. I've already called in back up and paramedics." *blip*

Paramedics! My heart ceased its rapid beating. *Please,* I prayed. *Let Coach be okay.* I listened on.

"Ok, what's your location Officer Canatelli? We will come to you." *blip.*

"Approximately two hundred and fifty steps northeast of the residence's business establishment, above the water's edge." *blip.*

"Roger." *blip.*

Officer Davis unclipped the loop that held her gun in place so that it was at the ready and retrieved a flashlight from her belt as well.

"Stay behind me at all times, and listen closely for any directions I may give you. Do not under any circumstances leave my side." I nodded my agreement to her commands. It was her duty to protect me, a civilian, I understood that. However I couldn't guarantee my impulses wouldn't get the best of me if I came across a horrific scene involving Coach. Feelings could not be governed in those kinds of situations. I braced myself for whatever may come.

We made our way out the front door and headed in the direction Officer Canatelli indicated. Officer Davis made full well I stayed behind her at all times. Her flashlight lit the way whilst her other hand shielded me from passing her. She shined her beam of light across our surroundings with each methodical step.

"Well, that appears to be how your perp was able to spy on you." She indicated towards a wooden box that had been drug from the woodshed to underneath the bedroom window. I recognized it to be the same box Coach had built in order to store his chopped wood for the fireplace during the winter months. It had been untouched and empty now for a few months as gathering season hadn't yet begun. The fresh soil and clumps of aged pine needles that now marked the pavement suggested the path in which the box had been drug. *That must have been the noise I heard prior to seeing the man's eyes,* I conceptualized. It sent shivers up my spine, knowing someone had gone to all the effort to watch through our window. *What all had he seen?*

Officer Davis trudged forth. I took only a moment longer, hugging myself for a bit of consolation before staggering after her once again. Passing the gym, then pushing through the trees that led to the clearing over above the water's edge. Realistically the walk would only normally take a few minutes, seconds even, but at that moment it felt like forever. When we finally emerged into the clearing, we could see Officer Canatelli's spotlight bouncing around in the near distance. Two shadowed outlines hovered around its vivid glow, and Officer Davis and I both instinctively broke into a jog. The urge to get there fast once again nagged at my gut. I could hear frustrated shouts carrying in the wind, cussing. Their looming figures turned to face us.

Officer Davis had her gun out now, and aimed it at the second silhouette. Officer Canatelli could easily be recognized as the first figure, with his hat and badge on and carrying the spotlight.

"It's ok, Deb, you can put that away." Officer Canatelli announced. Officer Davis lowered her weapon and re-holstered it.

"Are you okay?" I surged forward clutching Coach's rain soaked body to my chest. He did not return my embrace. I stepped back to look at him. His arms were pinned behind his back, his wrists cuffed.

"What's going on? Why are you in cuffs?" I looked from him to Officer Canatelli, waiting for someone to explain.

"Well, when I first came across them, they were fighting. He was on top of the other guy. For all I knew, he was the invader. So I separated them, and as I was cuffing him, he was trying to explain to me who he was. The other guy seemed like he was hurt, so I just assumed this guy was lying, trying to get me to release him. While I was distracted, the one on the ground rolled down the bank into the river and used the current to swim away before I even realized." I could tell Officer Canatelli was embarrassed admitting all of this. Coach was seething.

"You should have let me go as soon as I told you I was the landowner!"

"Well, we get a lot of folks who claim that once they've been caught, so I couldn't trust you right off the bat. Not to mention you were putting up a hell of a struggle. It's usually only the guilty ones that struggle the way you did." Coach eyed him up scornfully. He held his tongue, but I knew he wouldn't likely forgive.

"Why is he still in cuffs now then?" I questioned.

"Well I had radioed for backup and then responded to you amidst my fight with this one, but once he saw that the perp had escaped, he went ape shit. Started cussing me out, kicked my legs out from under me and everything. I had to tackle him down just to get him to stick around. I'm going to remind him now too, that I could charge him with battery of a police officer if he doesn't calm down." He shot Coach a threatening glare which Coach returned with fervor.

"You let him get away! You cuffed me and then allowed the actual culprit to escape! I was trying to do your job!"

"It is not the public's duty to apprehend intruders. I am also obligated to remind you that even though he may have entered your property without permission, if he did not strike at you first, then you may also be charged with assault if his identity becomes known. Self defense only applies if you've been struck first, and being a property owner doesn't give you the right to brutalize criminals these days. You need to walk a tightrope just like everyone else. If I hadn't been so distracted dealing with you, he wouldn't have had the opportunity to get away."

Coach shook his head defiantly and in disbelief, but said no more.

"Well, now that it's been sorted out that he is in fact not the perpetrator, can he be released now?" I looked from Officer Canatelli's face to Officer Davis's, as they exchanged looks.

"I think given his temper, perhaps we'll leave him as he is until after the backup arrives." Clearly Coach had pushed Officer Canatelli's limits.

When backup arrived, they spread out to do a search of the area to see if they could locate our offender, with no luck. The paramedics looked us all over, but as it was more welts than open wounds, it was a quick scan before leaving again. Officer Davis scribbled Coach's and Officer Canaetelli's statements on her notepad in order to do up their police report later on. Coach was finally un-cuffed and we were able to return to the house. His digital clock flashed its iconic red numbers at us that read 3:21AM. *So much for sleep.* I thought. Toweling off and slipping into some dry clothes, we slipped into bed. We had checked all the doors again and every room just to be sure we were indeed alone. His gun was positioned within reach beside the bed, just in case.

Snuggling into him, we both wrapped our arms around each other's chilled bodies in an attempt to warm up. I wanted to talk about what had happened, let him vent his frustrations, but I was in such a daze, and the weight of sleep fell heavy on my eyelids now that the adrenaline had finally left my body. My body went slack, and before I even had time to dream, I jerked awake to the sound of the alarm alerting us it was the start of another day.

18

Coach

What a fiasco! I couldn't believe the happenings that night had brought. The police offered to do nightly drive bys to help us feel safer for the time being and hopefully prevent the tom from returning. Personally, I felt I'd prefer them not doing their drive bys. *Let him come back,* I thought. He'd pay for it the next time.

Sleep deprivation once again marred my day. Paige had left for work that morning. I wasn't sure where she was scrounging the energy from. I had drug myself out of bed and decided to return to where I could find some happiness and not dwell on things.

I punched in the code on the lock's pin-pad. The light turned green allowing me entry, and I swung out the door. A faint smile crept across my face as I began instantly reminiscing about our activities in the room. I couldn't wait until our next kinky rendezvous.

I began tidying up, sanitizing, wiping things down, and putting the toys away. That's when I saw it. In the far corner, buried in the shadows, a crumpled up piece of fabric. I knew for a fact it hadn't been there when I assembled the room and had readied it for Paige's and my first round of exploration, prior to me initially showing her the room and her hesitation. I slunk back into the corner and knelt to pick it up. The room's faded ambience was too dark for me to really discern what I held.

I stepped out into the luminous gym's lighting and examined the contents of my hand closely. It appeared to be some kind of kerchief. A sheer square of fabric with a familiar pattern on it. I thought hard. *Where did I know this pattern from?* The turquoise, gold, and aubergine paisleys burned into my brain as I searched my memory, trying to spot the vivid fabric. That's when it hit me... *Oh shit!*

Class was about to start, and the kids and their parents were all pouring in. Some already in their gis, some headed to the changerooms while the parents all found their usual locations in the spectator seats.

The gym buzzed with commotion as all the various conversations were being had, folks catching up and kids socializing or playing before class commenced.

As I stepped onto the mats, ready to teach, the gym fell silent. All conversations came to a halt abruptly, and the children all ran to line up against the wall, awaiting my instructions. I ran them through our warm up drills and some games before getting into the lesson for the day. As the class sat down to begin, the gym doors swung open. I didn't even need to look up to know who it was. Notoriously late, Kyle and Sophie ran in, their gis already on, and took their seats.

Becky Carlyle's eyes locked on mine as she gave a not so subtle wink, her mouth gaping open and her renowned wad of gum wedged in her teeth. Darting my eyes away as fast as possible, I attempted to hide the embarrassed flush that I felt redden my cheeks and avoided all eye contact from that incidental second, onward.

I began the directive on the Omoplata, first demonstrating with, then without a partner, explaining the movements and so forth before pairing them up to practice.

Class went on as it normally would, although the incessant lip smacking as that wad of gum was rolled and chewed ingrained in my ears, creating a vexing tick. The veins in my temples were pounding. I swore my ears twitched each time I heard her thickly painted lips poppysmic, which was an inordinate amount of times. My temperament rose with each *shmuck*. The humidity in the air continued to rise as the grappling portion of class had set in motion. I turned on my large shop fans to help disperse the muggy heat. Their consistent hum helped to drown out Becky's nagging voice as she drawled on, gossiping amongst her gaggle of girlfriends.

The end of class drew near, and I could feel her eyes boring into my back, I knew there would be words. She at least waited until the crowd had dispersed and excused Kyle and Sophie outside until she was ready to join them before closing in on me.

"So...round three?" She smiled, scrunching her nose in that irritating manner she always did.

"Not on your life." I grumbled while un-pocketing her kerchief and tossing it at her. Her bare neck had been the indicator that I was indeed correct in presuming Rebecca Carlyle was in fact the mysterious woman I had blackout sex with only a few nights before.

"Aw, why not? We had such a good time, and you were more than eager when you called me up that night." She gave me an overzealous open mouthed wink. I shuddered.

"That was a drunken mistake. It won't happen again." Her face turned a muddy red from the blend of her horrible fake tan and the anger rising in her cheeks.

"I gave you everything you wanted. I only just started walking right again, you kinky bastard!"

"Well, my apologies. It never should have happened. I'd blame the booze, but there were more factors at play that night as well." I stated matter of factly whilst thinking about my feelings that night. I thought Paige had left me forever. I thought she'd been so freaked out when she found out what kind of stuff I was into that she'd decided she'd better get out while she still could.

"Yeah, you mentioned that hussy you've been boning that night. But if she wasn't willing to please you in any way you liked, why on Earth is she even a factor now?"

"She is not a hussy!" My voice raised. I wasn't about to have anyone besmirch her good name on my account. She'd been amazing to me. I had just been too idiotic to see it.

"That's none of your business either." I asserted.

"Well, you made it my business that night when you told me all about it as you nailed me in that swing of yours. I still have the markings on my ass from that tawse to prove it too." *Was she hinting at blackmailing me with that remark?*

"Again, I was under the influence. It's over now."

"Ohhh, I don't know about that exactly." Her voice tantalized.

"What do you mean? It is. That was the last time. It should have never happened."

"Listen...Coach, if you don't want the illustrious Paige Bryant to find out about our recent excursion, then you're at my beck and call from now on."

Shit, what all had I told her? Why would I give her Paige's name like that? Becky must have recognized the stunned look on my face.

"Oh you told me A LOT! To say the least...If I were you, I'd reconsider your words, Coach."

Yep, I was being blackmailed...again. Fuck.

18.5
Becky

It was late when my phone started ringing. I had been having a smoke and watching a rerun of Sex in the City. The kids were at their dad's, so I had the house to myself. Normally I would have gone out, had a few drinks, socialized, but that night I just hadn't felt up to it. Perhaps the events to follow had been fate.

"Hello?"

"He..hello? Is this Becky?" It was Coach, and he sounded half drunk.

"Yes, Coach, to what do I owe the pleasure of this call?"

"I, uh, uh wanna show you something."

"That's pretty vague. What exactly do you want to show me at this hour?" I could tell for sure then that he was intoxicated. The slur of his voice and the rambling manner was a dead giveaway. I was going to enjoy toying with him. It suited my mood. Perhaps our night at the club made a better impression than I thought. Why else would he be calling me at that hour?

"Can't tell you on the er...phone. You gotta come here."

I told him it would cost him my cab fare to his place. I didn't have the cash on me and why not make him pay since he wanted this.

"Oohkay, sure."

I told him I'd see him shortly and called him a studmuffin. And with that I hung up the phone, with a devilish grin on my face. I knew he'd come around, just took the right circumstances, liquid circumstances.

My cab pulled up. Coach was sitting on one of the cement barricades in front of the gym, a beer in hand. He took another long swig before standing up tipsily and staggering over to pay the cabby. Even hammered drunk, and reeking of beer, he still made my loins quiver with desire.

"Well honey, you got me here now. What exactly did you want to show me?" I asked him and tried to hide my amusement at his drunken state. This was going to be fun. I wonder if he will even remember any of it.

The cab drove away and Coach waved his hand, motioning me to follow him. He led me to the gym, teetering and tottering the whole way, unable to avoid stepping in a large pile of mud as he went. I circled around it, steering clear of the mud, I wasn't about to get my new purple prada pumps filthy. I had taken some time to primp prior to hailing my cab and had chosen purple as my focal color for the night. I thought it highlighted the eggplant color in my neckerchief. I paired it with a skin tight purple ruched dress and black and silver sequined crop jacket. I always loved to draw attention.

The sound of my heels clicking on the flooring, his drunken scuffling, and my silver bangle bracelets clanging together were the only sounds. They echoed off the gym walls, filling all the empty space where a bunch of bustling bodies usually occupied. That night however, the only bodies were ours.

Almost falling over, he had to lean on the wall to maintain his balance in order to punch in a code on a security pin pad alongside the mysterious door from which I had seen him and Connie Cooper emerge a few months ago. I had yearned to know what secrets this secluded room held since then. It seemed I would finally find out.

With a subtle *click*, a faded amber glow procured from the ornate side mounted lights, casting the room and its embellishments in its soft gleam. My eyes couldn't take it all in at once, although I tried. The many oils and lubes, toys and pleasure tools completely overwhelmed my eyes. They darted this way and that, consumed with the multitude of provocative thoughts their presence invoked.

"Nice collection you got here." I commented. He'd held out on me our first time together. I did not expect he was into so much kink. My loins were thrilled at the sight! I must have given him the sexual awakening he needed during our first encounter.

"Ya, reeealy think so?" He slurred again. His eyes merely slits, I wasn't even sure if he could even see at that point. A more responsible woman probably would have put him to bed and waited for him to sober up, but I really didn't feel like being responsible. I wanted to indulge in this man's intoxicating essence once more. I doubted I'd get a chance again while he was sober. May as well take advantage of all he offered. The man was hung like a damned horse and knows how to use it!

I pounced on him. Jumping onto him, latching my lips on his and wrapping my legs around his waist. I wanted him to know there would be no guessing, we were getting nasty!

He reefed his face away and dropped me down, a gesture I thought would indicate he was going to turn me down. Instead he ripped off my clothes and then pushed me down to my knees. Unzipping his fly, his abundant manhood sprung forth eager for my mouth to take him. And take him I did!

I shoved his girthy length down my throat, slathering him with saliva, choking on him repeatedly, letting him feel my throat close tight around his shaft. I watched him while I went down on him, his head tossing back, running his fingers through his hair, fisting mine and bobbing me up and down on his knob. Sucking him hard like a hoover vacuum, and tongue twirling his shroom like a cherry tootsie pop, I could hear him groaning in rapture. Cowper's fluid poured from him, strings of it formed from his glans to my lips as I continued to suck him off. I was wet, tasting the evidence of his arousal. Knowing that I was the one turning him on so much, making him so rigid and dripping. In fact, I relished it.

Without a moment's notice, he guided me up by my hair, not harshly, but more of a soft tug, using it as a bridle and reins. Using my neckerchief he quickly knotted up my hair and then looped it onto the closest hook that suspended the hanging sex chair in the air. I had to stand on my tip toes, otherwise I too would have been nearly suspended by it. Little did I know at that moment, that was his plan. He hoisted my naked body up and stood back, pulling my hair taut. Then he vigorously slammed his cock into me. An exalted squeal escaped my lips, and I heard him release a throaty grunt as he began heaving in and out of me as I hung there by the roots of my hair. His fingers dug into my ass cheeks gripping them tight, supporting the majority of my weight. He was thrusting so hard, giving me everything he had, filling me whole.

My double Ds made a heavy clapping sound each time they bounced off my chest, and my ass echoed that clap with every plunge in through my meat curtains. The sound effects only added to the thrill, heightening my arousal.

Hoisting a knee up and using that to help support my weight momentarily, he released his grip on my ass. With his one free hand he then began searching for something, all the while still pumping away. Dragging a contraption out of a darkened cubby, he slid it underneath me. I couldn't make out what it was, having my head bridled up the way it was. It was only my peripherals that had seen as much as I had been able to make out. He continued to bounce me up and down on his meat, never missing a beat, despite all his multi-tasking. He fiddled with yet another thing he grabbed off the shelf before setting it down again.

I tried to ignore what was going on and immersed myself once again in the pleasure being bestowed upon me, when suddenly his knee jolted out from under me and I catapulted down, my hair pulling on my head and his hands once again grasping my ass. He wasn't catching me though, the kinky bastard was splaying my cheeks apart and slammed my corn-hole down around a huge lubricated knob. I screamed!

He ignored my hollers and began shoving his weight down on me as he simultaneously pushed into me. His dick rubbed my g-spot as his weight pushed the knob further and further up inside me. The lube was my saving grace! It eased it in me just the way I liked it until my ass fully encompassed its girth. Then with a flick of his thumb, the contraption that was now completely submerged in my arse began jack hammering me from behind. He throttled the front, and the machine fucked my back.

My masochism tendencies were in full swing! It was exhilarating feeling my rear end being destroyed, my hair lifting off my scalp with the pressure as well as having his huge manhood boring into me. *SMACK!*

"Oh fuuuuuck yeah! Spank me again, Daddy!" The words tumbled out of my mouth, my lips quivering.

"It's Coach!" He grunted hoarsely, quickening his pace, throttling into me before winding up and spanking me again hard.

Liquor sweats drizzled down his temples and body. I could practically smell the whiskey and beer seeping out of his pores. If I could have reached his face, I would have licked the sweat right off of it; gotten drunk off his bodily discharge. Instead I felt the droplets spatter as they hit my thighs, and longed to taste them.

I could feel my clit swelling, his pubis stroking and tantalizing it each time he sunk his pole inside me.

I heard my own voice shriek that I was about to cum as my mind drifted off into an elevated space, everything disappearing aside from the continued pleasurable pounding I was taking in both holes. It consumed me, darkness blanketed my eyes, and I let go, releasing all my pent up exultations in one long vibrant wail!

I was a rag doll being fucked in the air, flaccid with enjoyment. Coach drilled on, pummeling my pussy, his face stone set and going red with exertion now. With orgasm number one down, my sensory receptors were beyond roused and indulging in every motion I was subjected to. I craved...more.

"Eat me, you bastard!" I shrieked at him venomously. He glared at me for a second, still thrusting away. Possibly contemplating, as he was so immersed in his art. I almost thought he might pull out and walk away, but he didn't. With an angry jolt, he whipped his meat out of me and plopped me down on the ground only long enough to bend me over and then lift me up again by my hip-line. My head hung, while my twat hovered in his face like a TV dinner, steamy and hot right after the seals had been ripped off it. Ready for him to gorge himself.

His mouth engulfed my snatch, wolfing it down like a salisbury steak sandwich. I don't paint the prettiest picture, but he was eating it like he had a huge appetite, which only stirred mine as well. Sixty-nining in the air, I stuffed his cock once again down my throat, gagging as his pole slid down the length of my throat, past my tonsils, surpassing my gag reflex. I thought for sure he was hovering past my trachea. He wanted it deep, deep I would give him. I continued sucking him, gagging on him with each dive down his lengthy pole. My lady juice was overflowing and beginning to drizzle down my abdomen, as he power munched the shit out of me. It was so fucking hot! Feeling him suck my labia, and swallow as much of me as he could. His grip never faltered around my hips, I knew I'd be sore later. And then... Orgasm number two!

I sputtered my intense pleasure at my impending orgasm around his dick still fully submerged in my mouth. He quivered tenaciously, feeling my vocal cords vibrate around his knob. He shifted and I knew he was ready to change positions once again, what did he have in store next, I wondered.

With an easy flip he had me upright again. The blood rushing to my toes left me feeling numb and tingly, perhaps even a bit light headed. But I had no time to process that before he was swinging me around and tethering my wrists to the wall. Pulling on a small strap that was embedded in the drywall, a padded shelf slid out of the wall. It resembled a miniature massage table and a tripod leg plopped out of the bottom of it, securing it to the floor, propping it up and supporting its weight. With my wrists now bound, he steered me forwards, causing me to kneel onto its tabletop like structure.

There I was, positioned now on all fours, shackled. As I was facing away from him, I could only feel as he secured yet two more straps around my ankles, fastening me to the shelf's surface. I was bound tight and completely at his mercy.

With an almighty heave, he once again thrust up inside me from behind. I at first thought it was going to be any old doggy style session, but I was much mistaken.

It started with a tickle, the sleek fabric of leather tassels being drug alongside my rear end and thighs...then caressing my spine while simultaneously being fucked. Goosebumps rose on my skin, sending shivers throughout my limbs. I bit my lip in anticipation, knowing full well, a light tickling was not going to be the extent of it.

Crack!

"Ahh!" I squealed as the leather stirrups slashed my skin. He had a Scottish tawse, and was not holding back. The heat from the initial whip site scorched my skin. The burning radiated down my lumbar into my thighs, when another *crack* lit my rear end on fire! It became a rhythmic pump and whip. Sometimes he'd elevate his pace and do multiple thrusts before slashing my back and ass again and again. Tears bled down my face. I both loved and hated it. The sting was unbearable. The agony each welt produced left my body quaking. And yet...I could feel my clit humming and swelling with pressure, aching to combust yet again.

"Ugh, I can't wait to unload this cannon on you!" His deep throaty voice declared fervently. His words were my final trigger. My knees began to buckle, my body quaking with pain and pleasure, the release so strong, like nothing I'd ever experienced before. It was mind-blowing.

He still hadn't blown his load yet, despite me having cum three times. I thought once I came he'd ease up on the pelting. Boy was I mistaken. He went harder, amping it up even more, whipping me again and again. I could barely utter more than a whimper as the floggings came in increased succession one after another.

I craned my head to look back and see why he was carrying on so. His face twisted in an anguished outraged expression. His brow was furrowed and violent, his thrusts also heated and hard. *Had I done something wrong?*

This was no longer fun. It had gone too far. I swore I could feel my back and rear swelling from the abundance of welts now veiling them. Tears streamed down my face, dripping on the shelf's leather upholstery. I felt like I had developed a fever, my forehead perspiring with the sheer pain I was being subjected to. Each time I tried to holler out for him to stop, another savage lash braised my raw skin and I could only manage to suck wind. Why had I not told him my safe word? I wondered in that moment if he even abided by that. I'd never felt the need to use it before even though I still had one. Kinky sex needs rules, boundaries and a sense of trust. I guess I forgot to establish all of those in my rush to get laid. For that mistake, I would pay.

A splatter of red appeared on my hand, I could see the drizzle of blood running down my shoulder and down my arm. With all my might, I heaved a grievous,

"WWwwhhhhyyyy?"

I collapsed onto my forearms, reduced to sobs. That's when he finally pulled out and shot his load all over my back. Hot cum stung all my many welts, and he breathed an exasperated sigh of relief as I continued to sob into the sweat soaked leather.

"Suh...sorry. Guess I got a little out of hand." I sensed that he just realized the extent of his actions, and felt the remorse in his words. I sniffed as he released me from my restraints, and I quickly wiped my tears. He retreated somberly from the room, giving me a moment to collect myself.

The searing pain on the backside of my body, which I breathed through, beared it, pushed it deep down, was slowly slipping away. My masochism was real. It had been the biggest reason my husband and I had split. He wasn't keen on how far I wanted to take it, couldn't understand that I loved it. Needed it. I craved the humiliation, the pain, the pleasure I got from that pain.

He never hit me as hard as Coach had though. He didn't have the capacity for it, nor the muscle. Plain sex was boring, I craved more. Now there I was, bloody with tear stained cheeks and a haunting buzz of adrenaline pumping through my engorged clit. I know I am fucked up, and I am okay with it.

I scanned the room, searching through all the cubbies before I found what I was seeking. I followed Coach out of the room, and found him sipping on a frosty cold beer from the gym's fridge. His taut muscular rear end glowed in the fridge's dim amber lighting. Hearing me approach, he turned around, giving me the full frontal view, and I gulped. My eyes explored his body greedily, and I felt the blood rush to my groin, hot with want all over again.

Being bold, I gave my flirtiest smile and walked up, stealing the beer from his hand and taking a long swig. I flicked the little foiled packet I had stuffed in my palm at him. He picked it up and seeing it was an ultra thin magnum, he looked at me confused.

"How about round two?" I smirked at his dumbfounded expression and sauntered back to the room, only looking back over my shoulder for a mere second to see his mouth twitch into a small relieved smile, eyes narrow and his fists clenched as he downed the rest of his beer before following me back through the doorway.

It was during the next round that he began to blabber about why he had called me in such an inebriated state. I got some great details on his private life. Connie Cooper was not the only one to get a shot with Coach. He'd been spending plenty of time coloring outside the lines with one of his students as well. Paige Bryant. That explained her one on one lessons. I still don't know what he saw in her that I couldn't offer, that I had not already offered him.

This new found detail would make for good leverage to use for another date later if necessary. It seems there was trouble in paradise though, and that little side gig might be over thanks to his true desires in the bedroom. Little Paige Bryant was apparently a lightweight. She wasn't as tough as her winning streak at jiu jitsu made her appear.

I could give him all he needed and more. I just need to make him see it. I will and he will love it even if I have to blackmail him again to get another chance. I could easily become addicted to this man.

19

Coach

The gym was abuzz. Rumors were floating ear to ear. Rebecca Carlyle was missing. From what I heard, her ex-husband had come home from his stint of work to get the kids from her sometime after our confrontation when I had given her back her neckerchief. The kids were home alone. They had no idea where she was. According to them, she had gone to grab groceries quickly and had left Kyle in charge. She never returned.

Her ex, Bill, arrived the next day and found she'd left for a quick grocery trip hours earlier and had not returned. Fortunately, they weren't alone for more than twelve hours. At ages nine and twelve, that was still a bit longer than they should have been by themselves.

Bill called their relatives, friends, and all her usual hot spots, but she was nowhere to be found. She may have been a wild one, but she was responsible with her kids and would never intentionally leave them for long. Certainly never for hours at a time, and the grocery store was less than ten minutes away on foot.

The cops were alerted and began a search. They got a warrant for the grocery store's cameras. However, being such a small community where she lived, there weren't many cameras, and the footage didn't pick up much. She was seen getting groceries like she claimed she was doing, but then once outside again, nothing.

My anxiety was eating away at me. Besides her kids, and a few witnesses at the grocery store, I had likely been one of the last people to have seen her...

Two weeks had passed since Becky's disappearance. The cops had no leads. Her kids hadn't been at class, understandably so, and the gym's spectator area was in a constant state of hush. The communities had all banded together to help with searches, and parents were keeping their kids much closer than usual out of fear. We began focusing on more self defense in classes, just to help ease parents' minds. I wanted them to know their kids were as prepared as they could be if something were to ever happen.

My five o'clock class had just begun, and we had completed warm up and were onto the lesson portion. I was demonstrating a rear naked choke when my attention was drawn to the door. Two cops in full gear walked in and quickly conversed with one of the parents, Chase Dhillon, who had been hovering near the door watching. I saw Chase respond and point in my direction. The cops nodded and started walking in my direction.]

I instructed my students to partner up in order to practice before I made my way to meet them, assuming it was my turn to be questioned.

"Coach?"

"Yes, that's me, how can I help you gentlemen?"

"You are under arrest for the murder of Rebecca Lee Carlyle. You have the right to remain silent. Anything you say can and will be used against you in a court of law. You have the right to an attorney. If you cannot afford an attorney, one will be provided for you."

The cop in the lead read me my miranda rights as the second circled around me and gruffly secured my wrists whilst cuffing me.

"What's this all about?" I demanded, completely aghast.

"We have recovered Rebecca Carlyle's body. There is evidence connecting you to her murder.

"That's preposterous!" I snarled.

The gym had fallen silent. All the onlookers' eyes gaped at me. Parents grabbed their children and hugged them close, now believing their children had been in danger in my presence.

"The evidence is pretty inarguable at this point. We have a warrant to bring you in. Come on, don't make more of a scene than you have already." A rough shove from behind caused me to stagger forwards.

I hated to admit it, but he was right. I didn't want to make more of a scene. This was bad enough for business and my reputation. I lowered my gaze to avoid eye contact and allowed myself to be led outside to the squad car awaiting me.

20

I sat in that cell for days. Completely alone, isolated. Left with nothing but my thoughts. I had the opportunity to speak with my lawyer, but he wasn't much help. He encouraged me to cooperate, and he could maybe get the charges eased, but his idea of "eased" was a joke as well. From life down to twenty years with no chance of parole. My gut was in utter knots. I wasn't sure how they had even come to these conclusions, or off of what evidence they were basing all this.

I kept going over what I had told them, again and again. I didn't understand why my story was so hard to believe, or where they were getting their facts from. They had also charged me with yet another murder... a man whose existence I had denied for years. A man, who I hadn't even seen since my childhood. My father.

The investigator who interrogated me revealed that Becky had been asphyxiated. They had found her body a few kilometers down current from the grocery store she was last sighted at in Celista. They originally thought she had drowned, but the coroner ruled that out and ordered an autopsy. The local authorities had brought in a search and rescue team with dogs, and the dogs had managed to sniff her out.

The autopsy showed a large hematoma across her windpipe, it resembled similar markings to that of ones caused by a rear naked choke.

They also discovered lashes all over her back and buttocks. They believed the source of these was some form of leather whip. Apparently, there was also DNA evidence that matched my own. Seminal remnants embedded in a few of the gashes, and evidence of rough intercourse, including rubber latex residue in her vagina.

Fuck my life.

They fingerprinted me as per their usual write up routine and with my lawyer insisting once again that I cooperate. They also took swabs of my cheeks to analyze at the lab. I couldn't explain her death, or the bruise, or even the welts, all I remembered was waking up with a used condom on my dick the next morning and being extremely hung over. But they didn't buy my story, and now with my DNA confiscated, I was sure it was only a matter of time before I was behind bars for life.

It had to be all circumstantial. I didn't think I'd ever be capable of doing the things I was being accused of. I could only hope that the evidence would prove my innocence, that another man was with her prior to her disappearance. That I wasn't the one that had marked her up so bad, and that someone else knew jiu jitsu and suffocated her. But even going over it in my mind, it seemed less and less likely.

My heart sank...as much as I'd like to believe she was with another guy in that short of a timeline. I had some serious doubts, which only meant bad news for me. Once it was confirmed to be my semen, I was done for.

I hadn't spoken to Paige since the morning I was arrested. I don't think she had any way of knowing I was imprisoned. I had used my one phone call to get ahold of my mother. She of course was worried sick and was preparing to make the flight back to Canada in order to come support me. I preferred she didn't. I didn't want her to have to bear my shame. But she'd never not come, not when it could mean her son ending up behind bars.

As for the other murder, I wasn't sure how I'd even been pegged guilty for that one. I hadn't even seen the man since I was a child for Christ's sake! Apparently he was killed in a similar fashion, and that was the main reason I was brought in for it. It seemed someone was becoming a bit of a serial killer. Perhaps one of my students, although I could never narrow it down to who. Everyone I taught seemed so genuine. Otherwise, I wouldn't be teaching them. I would have weeded them out the way I usually did with any bad eggs in my groups, like Greg. Wait! Greg!

Could this be revenge for the way I treated him all those months ago? He had perfected his skills and now was framing me to get back at me? Was he that low? That evil? I may have been grasping at straws, but it was all I had. A false sense of hope.

How would he have known who my father was though? Or my connection to Becky? Doubt once again ravaged my thoughts.

I laid on my concrete bed, staring at the ceiling, focusing on all the scratch marks where prisoners before me had managed to use either their nails or sporks to carve their names, initials, or some sort of profanities into it. Someone had even kept count of the number of days they had been incarcerated. There were numerous tally marks that marred the ceiling and walls...

"Hey! Look alive in there, you have a visitor." The guard's voice snapped my attention back.

"A visitor?"

He beckoned me over. I had to turn around and stick my wrists through the bars to allow him to cuff me prior to him opening the door. He guided me down the hall to the visitor corridor, where being deemed a dangerous murderer, I was once again locked in a private cell. This one had cement walls on all sides, not adjoining cells.

It was too early for my mother to have arrived, but she was the only one who knew I was in here that would come to visit. With my reputation now defamed, I didn't expect to see anyone besides her.

Escorted by yet another cop, Paige walked in. He pulled up a chair for her and told her he'd be back in approximately twenty minutes. I could see her bat her doe eyes at him, convincing him to let her have a few more minutes.

"Fine, thirty minutes then." He gave her a subtle smirk, checking out her rear end before turning and leaving the cell block.

"I didn't know they were allowing conjugal visits." I joked playfully, trying to make light of the situation. Her eyes told me my ploy had not worked. She hurried over to meet me at the bars and wrapped her arms around me through them. A hug was exactly what I needed in that moment. Being within her warm embrace, to hear her heart so close. I breathed her in, smelling her hair before releasing a long drawn out sigh. Moments passed before I broke the silence.

"I'm innocent, Paige."

"I know you are." Her embrace tightened. Squeezing me desperately.

"But it doesn't matter now..." Slightly confused by the tail end of her comment, I brushed it off. I took it to mean she loved me anyway despite the situation.

"I don't know what to do." I confessed, my voice finally cracking.

"I need to prove my innocence, but I'm not sure how to do that." I admitted ruefully. She pulled back, looking up at me, her eyes blinking away her emotions. *My tough girl, always afraid to show her vulnerability.*

"I don't want to be without yo-..." Her finger pressed against my lips, silencing me before I could finish.

"No talking." She whispered before lifting up her leg and sticking it through the bars, wrapping it around me and pulling my hips in provocatively.

"Babe, I'm literally locked in a cell right now. There are guards everywhere."

My words were lost on her. She wasn't listening. Instead she was fiddling with my zipper, unveiling my manhood which despite my verbal protests, was stiffening quickly.

"I was joking about the conjugal visit you know." She didn't laugh, she kept at it.

She was wearing a jean mini skirt, with two well placed slits on either side of her thighs that enabled her to spread her legs. A feature I was quite elated about. Her v-neck camisole and lace brasserie showed off her bosoms. I wished I could grab them, touch her, do anything really. But being cuffed with my hands behind my back, I was useless and at her mercy. I hated to admit it, but it was kind of a turn on, especially when I realized she wasn't wearing any panties.

My erection now bulged, to which she smiled and bit her bottom lip, pleased with her attire's, or the lack thereof, efficacy on me. Retrieving my rigid shaft from my prison jumpsuit, she began jerking me off with one hand and touching herself with the other. Her eyes locked on mine, she wanted me to watch her, wanted to be my hands.

I couldn't help myself, I kept nervously glancing at the door, afraid at any second we'd be caught. My adrenaline ran high, adding to my excitement. Feasting my eyes on her as she pleasured herself. Hearing every shuddered breath, every soft moan, and her wetness growing, only caused me to want her more. I began to get lost in her eyes, her beauty was hypnotizing.

With no warning, she hooked her leg, pulling me in tighter and guided my cock inside her.

"I don't want to waste any time." She explained as she started bouncing up and down on me, grinding her pussy down on my knob. She gripped the bars for balance, and using all her strength, she hoisted herself up into the air as if I were holding her. With the steel partition between us, she fucked me. Pulling herself up and down, her vagina gliding down my shaft. I rolled my head back in pure ecstasy.

I wanted nothing more than to hold her, touch her, feel her whole body one last time. If only. The minutes were precious. I wasn't even sure how much time we had left, but she was determined to make me forget about the time. Her breasts jounced methodically with her humping. My eyes were directly aligned with them. I got to take them all in, appreciate their voluptuous curves and her gorgeous brown skin. *God I loved this woman.*

She lowered herself to the ground, kissed me passionately, then pulled me out only long enough to turn around before pushing her behind into my crotch. My dick slipped back inside her well lubricated cunt, and she pulsated back and forth, letting me watch myself slip in and out of her. Seeing all her gloss painted up and down my shaft, her labia pulled so tight around it, just the visual was enough to make me want to blow my load.

I began heaving into her, matching her rhythm. Slamming my head inside her, her muscular ass jostling with each hefty thrust. My hips hitting the steel bars each time we made contact, the sound echoed off the cement walls. She bent right down, touching her toes, and that's when I could hold it in no longer. Her clam clenched down on me, gripping my meat tightly, causing me to thrust faster and harder, my climax peaking. I couldn't pull out, there was nowhere for me to shoot my cum without making a suspicious mess. I came in her, filling her hole. Jizz bubbled around the base of my dick as I leaned my forehead on the cool bars panting.

"I...I'm sorry, I couldn't pull out." She giggled at me.

"That's ok, I didn't want you to." She stepped forward, my pole still rigid and covered in spunk, flopped out of her. Using her hand she wiped the remaining fluids off me and licked her hand, swallowing the remnants before stuffing me back inside and zipping my jumpsuit back up.

"Well, now that that's out of the way..."

"But, you didn't orgasm yet, I don't want to leave you unsatisfied."

"I'm never unsatisfied when I'm with you. That's why this is so hard."

"I know babe, I'm sorry about all of this." I hung my head, remorse dripping with every word. That's when I made up my mind, it was now or never...

"Paige, I never thought myself capable of finding someone I cared for so much. You've changed me, for the better. This isn't how I planned to do this, but I don't want you going through life thinking I didn't want to spend the rest of my life with you. I love you, Paige Bryant. Will you do me the honor of being my wife?" I kneeled down, my arms still pinned behind me, but my eyes held hers as I asked the question that had been weighing on my mind for weeks now. I knew I had fucked up, a lot. I hadn't treated her fairly, but I wanted nothing more than to spend the rest of my life making it up to her, even if it meant I'd be doing it from prison.

She stared at me, a stunned expression affixed on her face. I had clearly taken her by surprise.

"I'm sorry, I know what I'm asking and that this isn't the ideal proposal or situation. I just can't imagine going through this life without you. Perhaps I'm being selfish. I just thought, if we were married, you could take over the gyms, keep them going, train. Live your dream. And hopefully, one day, I'll get out of here and we can run them together."

"Austin, I'm pregnant."

"What?" My mouth gaped open, and I stared at her in disbelief.

"Well, we weren't exactly using protection."

"I just thought you were on the pill."

"Well, that's not a hundred percent effective either, but no. I was never on birth control, I hadn't exactly been overly sexually active for a period before you. I despised most men."

I exhaled audibly. I was struggling to process the new information she had bestowed upon me...I was going to be a father.

"I have to prove that I'm innocent, Paige. I can't not be an involved father to our child."

"You can't prove you're innocent either."

"Well, I know the evidence seems pretty solid right now, but I know I didn't kill either Becky or my dad. I haven't even seen my dad since I was a child. How on Earth could I have murdered him? And for what reason?"

"I'm not doubting that you didn't do it, but I'm saying you can't prove you didn't..."

"It'll be hard, but I have to try!"

"It's impossible."

"What do you mean? Nothing's impossible, babe. We just have to have faith." I didn't blame her for feeling disheartened, so I was trying my best to reassure her.

"Yes it is, especially with all the evidence against you."

"Wait, what evidence are you speaking of exactly?" My curiosity piqued as I didn't know she was even aware as to much of the reason I was arrested let alone what evidence was involved.

"Well, for starters, the fact that it's your abusive father who is dead, all the whip marks on Rebecca Carlyle's back that match the Scottish tawse in your secret sex room? Or perhaps the seminal deposits that you left both in her and in the used rubber I found in your garbage can? Or maybe your thumbprint bruises imprinted above her hips? Oh, then there's the well versed graphic details she wrote, journaling all of your extracurricular activities together both in the past and as of recently. Or maybe... it was the neckerchief on the floor of your sex room that I then saw on her orange tinted neck later on. I don't imagine there's too many of those floating around in one small town. Take your pick." Her voice was filled with malice, her face stone cold and set. There was no emotion anymore. I gawked at her, realization dawning on me, but I asked anyway.

"Paige...how do you know all of that?"

She continued to stare me down, then cracked her neck casually, refusing to answer me.

"It was you...wasn't it? You killed them?"

"Well of course it was me! I killed your repulsive father after I figured out it was him snooping around your house at night, spying on us. Turns out he had been watching you for a while. It took me a bit to clue in, but then when I saw him again outside your gym smoking, I connected the dots. He was the one I'd seen before, watching through the glass at your gym, then lurking in the bedroom window at night. I could smell the cigarettes on him when he knocked me down in the woods that night, and I felt his arm hair. Plus, he does look like you, just harder to recognize it since he's grown a beard. He also perfectly matched the description of the older man watching you and that whore Becky Carlyle fucking that she wrote about in her journal. It was you he was watching, not me. Guess he saw your picture in the paper and tracked you down."

That all made so much sense now. It was me he was observing when he was watching during my classes, not the kids, like I had originally thought. No wonder he had been so disgusted at my accusation.

"But, why did you kill him?"

"I killed him out of empathy for you, after what he put you through, all your pain. Beating your mom like that, making you ashamed of your own name. He had to go. I did you a favor." She truly believed she had done a good deed. She didn't even try to hide her pride. Her nose was up in the air and her chest puffed haughtily. At one time, I probably would've agreed with her, that it was a favor if he was gone, a blessing even. But I never wished him to be murdered. I was fine living my life the way I was, without him, and doing better, helping kids and adults alike to not be victims.

"What about Becky? You were jealous? Because I only did it to protect my reputation and gym the first time, the second was because I was black out drunk. I was devastated when you walked out on me that day after I revealed the room to you. I thought you didn't want to be with me, I seriously thought you'd ended things and left. I was mourning in the only way I knew how, to numb myself."

"I was not JEALOUS." She spat at me venomously.

"I killed her because you were supposed to be MINE! I don't share! I had to kill that whore, once I found out you'd fucked her. I couldn't let her live! Especially when she was threatening to release that kind of info. No one was ever going to find out you cheated on me with that old disgusting heifer!"

"I get you were mad, but we could have talked about it! You didn't need to kill her! This is insanity. Paige, you're going to end up in prison, over something so stupid!"

"Like hell I am. I'm not going down for their murders. I could've easily gotten rid of their bodies like I did the others, but I wanted them to be found. I knew you'd be found guilty for it, and I'd be off scott free."

I was completely floored. My gut was in knots so tight I couldn't have even thrown up. Even though the desire to do so was very much there.

"What do you mean, the others, Paige?"

"Ugh, quit calling me that! My name's not Paige. I'm so sick of this alias. My name is Elisha, Elisha Delano. Perhaps you've heard of me?"

The name had in fact struck a bell...Elisha Delano was a notorious serial killer. I had heard her name along with a list of her alias identities repeated on the radio and news often. I had never paid that much attention when her photos had been broadcasted in her many disguises though, or I'm sure I would have eventually noticed. That is probably why she seemed so familiar to me when we first met. It was likely because I had seen all her disguises broadcasted on the Most Wanted ads. I had to hand it to her, it would be hard to hide a face that beautiful, and yet I hadn't caught on.

She killed every man she ever got involved with, all under those different aliases. I wasn't sure if they had scorned her, if she did it for money, or perhaps her sheer lust for blood. That's when the full realization hit me. *I had trained a serial killer...to be even deadlier.*

"Why me? Why did you choose me?"

"You were the only man who was my equal, my match. Your strength and fake facade. I thought perhaps there was more to you as well, a story like my own. Then as I got to know you, I discovered you were just a compassionate fool. I almost couldn't go through with murdering you...until you fucked around on me. Then you were just another disposable piece of garbage like the rest of them.

But then I found out I was pregnant. It was much more fun to pin these murders on you and get to watch you rot behind bars than it was to just kill you. Don't worry though, I will raise this baby to be strong, with a real spine. Not weak like you."

She wasn't lying about the pregnancy...I could see it in her eyes. The rest I was in sheer disbelief. I had been had. And it was my own undoing. My drunken mistake had cost me three lives. Rebecca Carlyle's, my estranged father's, and now...my own. I'd rot in jail for likely the remainder of my days.

"Aren't you afraid I'll turn you in? Tell them it was you? Now that you've divulged all your truths to me."

"You'd never."

"Why wouldn't I?"

"Because, I have your spawn in my belly."

She was right. I'd never risk anything happening to that baby. I'd endure the years, just to protect my little seedling from both his mother...and the truth.

As the reality of what I had to do sank in, I was forced to acknowledge; we all had an eminence front. It wasn't just me. If I had faced things, re-connected or sought out my father, owned my name again, then perhaps he'd still be here. Becky might still be here, and her children would still have their mother.

Epilogue

"And here I am now, Doctor. On your couch summarizing my life."

"Yes, however, you still have yet to tell me exactly, who you are? I have a referral for you, Mr. Wilkinson, yet it includes very little information, not even your first name. I have never come across such a vague document as this before. Especially when referred from the judicial system. Please, enlighten me." Dr. Rudolph Bragg sat there, laid back on his black leather seat, clipboard in hand.

His pen had been scratching notes the entire time I unraveled my story to him. However, now he leaned forward with a genuine interest, his pen at a standstill, and a look of general curiosity upon his face. His peppered mustache curled on each end landing just shy of his glasses that had slid down his nose, perching just on its tip.

I took a deep breath, and tried to focus on a focal point in order to finally reveal my emotional truth. I stared at Dr. Bragg's redwood door, its fogged glass pane which had his name and occupation etched into the glass:

Dr. R.Bragg- Psychiatrist

I stared hard at those words, spelt backwards from my position, and took a deep breath again.

"My name is Austin Wilkinson. I prefer Coach. My mother was Naomi Finstead. She reverted back to her maiden name when my siblings and I graduated high school. My father was Chad Wilkinson. He abused my mother when I was a child and spent many years in prison following him breaking his restraining order." I explained in monotone.

"I hadn't heard from him most of my life after that, until I moved back here. That's when I noticed the strange older man following me and watching me at my gym.

I didn't want to see or hear from him again, but then he took that choice away from me when he confronted me at my house during the night. And you know the rest of that story." I turned my face to look at the doctor. So far, it seemed he was buying my bullshit with some truth thrown in.

"I watched my aunt commit suicide in front of me, shortly before we moved to Greece to escape all the pain and start fresh. It was my mother's way of remedying what we'd all gone through. Saving us all the shame of my father's actions and herself the guilt and heartache of my aunt's death."

"Forgive me, but why then did you return to the Shuswap? If your mother had moved you to Greece to give you a new and better life, why come back?"

"That's a good question, doc. I wondered myself. I guess I had it in my mind that I needed to make a new name for myself and right his wrongs. Give kids a safe place to vent, and also learn to protect themselves and others. I figured I needed to start it where it all happened, almost my own form of therapy, just like jiu jitsu." I shrugged and returned my gaze to the windowed door.

"I've never wanted to be called by my legal name because of him. I've always despised being called Austin Wilkinson. I wanted to change my name, but I also didn't want to hurt my mother's feelings. That's why I go by Coach. My siblings also had to grow up living with the name too, so I couldn't just trade mine in for another. We all share the burden his last name carries. Well, all but my little brother." I palmed my forehead, wiping the beads of nervous perspiration that had begun to form.

"I see. You took the trauma of your mother's abusive episode inflicted by the hand of your father, and have manifested it into fuel for your entire life. Your position as a coach, your training and passion for jiu jitsu, and the hate of your own name. I admire your drive and the way you handled your emotions as a young lad, turning something so awful into something so inspiring for so many others. You have quite a big heart, Coach, which I will attest to in court on your behalf."

"Thank you, Dr. Bragg."

"Why did you kill him though?"

"The hate took over me when I found him outside my home and finally realized who he was I guess. All I felt was sheer hatred. He came in the night. He had been sneaking around my home. I viewed it as a threat and went temporarily insane, I guess."

"Hmm..."

His pen scratched down on his pad once again.

"And what about in regard to Ms. Carlyle? Why did you feel the need to dispose of her life?"

"She threatened to bring down my business, ruin my reputation, my relationship. I had worked too hard, given up too much. I couldn't allow it."

He peered at me, I'm sure thinking exactly what I was when I concocted this falsehood. *How was this any reason to murder someone?* Obviously, I did not reveal to him the details of Paige's aka Elisha's confession to me.

"I do have one more question for you,"

"What's that?"

"You mentioned your siblings a few times throughout your story, yet I don't think you've ever mentioned having a brother before this moment?"

I took another big breath, *shit.*

"That's another long story, doc."

"I'm all ears, please go on." He sunk back into his chair, waiting.

I sighed and began.

"Prior to my father beating my mum, she had started a relationship with a really nice guy. He was a cop.

That's what triggered my dad to hurt her, his jealous rage, despite the fact they'd been separated for some time already at that point. She eventually recovered, and the guy and her were together for a short while.

He was really good to us kids, paid attention to us, spent time with us, all the things a father *should have* done." I nearly smiled at the pleasant memory, but quickly lost the moment as I continued the abbreviated version of that part of my life.

"He wasn't around long though. He and my father got into it at the beach that day, beating each other up in the beach parking lot. My mum managed to break them up, but that's also when my aunt jumped in front of the police car.

He ended up being detained along with my dad. My mother never did disclose to us why. While he was still locked up or receiving therapy for something, I can't quite remember, we left for Greece." I shrugged one shoulder as though it didn't much matter at this point.

"Anyway, a few months later, my mum gave birth to my younger brother. There was a pretty big age gap between all of us, and to be honest, I don't think any of us ended up being very close with him.

He had a different dad, he looked different than us, acted different, and he was a bit of a handful for mum."

I tried to hide the guilt I felt for my resentment. It wasn't his fault he was created.

"She wasn't expecting to have another baby, and she had no support for him either. I don't know, I guess Aeda, Everley, and I all resented him a bit. It wasn't fair to him, and we know that. I feel super guilty for it now, but I can't change the past. I don't even know where he is now. He took off. Mum keeps an ear out for him, hopes he'll return. I guess we'd all do the same thing."

I shrugged, and squirmed in my seat a bit. The fresh guilt created a clamminess that caused me to stick to the leather chaise.

"Thank you for disclosing this to me. I can see it was hard for you." Dr. Bragg's narrowed eyes, looked me up and down, scanning my visual signs of emotion, and obviously noting my sudden flush and clammy demeanor.

"Well, I think that is about it for the day, Austin. May I call you Austin?" I gulped and gave a short nod, knowing I'd have to face people calling me by my actual legal name starting in court in the following weeks. Best to get used to it now.

"I will get my write up done, and submit it to the judge and lawyers prior to next week's court proceedings. I appreciate you being so open with me. It will serve you well in trial." He gave me a short lip curl, likely his attempt at a smile. Any sign of warmth was welcome at this point. I needed all the empathy and compassion I could derive.

"Thank you, doctor." I began to get up as Dr. Bragg waved the guards in. They began uncuffing me from a steel pole that had been cemented in the office.

Clearly Dr. Bragg saw a lot of prisoner patients. The pole was subtle at least. It presented as a lamp, and to the untrained eye, would likely pass as one just lacking a lampshade.

The guards appeared eager to escort me back to the transport truck.

Dr. Bragg was observing his notes when his eyes darted up, acknowledging me one last time.

"What is his name?"

I looked over my shoulder at him questioningly, a guard on either side of me holding me steady. They paused to allow me to answer.

"Whose?"

"Your brother's."

I paused in the doorway, unsure why this was relevant to his assessment. I didn't like to disclose more information than I needed to, ever. But when my silence went on longer than a normal pause, one of the guards gave me a heave from behind, signaling me to answer.

I hesitated a moment longer and then heard my own voice stammer,

"Seth. His name is Seth Trail."

Prologue

My legs were pressing so hard in the stirrups I could feel my flesh bruising on impact. Sweat dripped down my face, as I grimaced in pain and effort.

It was only a few short months ago I had discovered I was in fact pregnant again with my fourth child. I had been approximately three months along when I took the time to acknowledge it. I thought just maybe, I'd been so stressed, with relocating, the funeral, starting a new life, selling our house etcetera, that I had just skipped a few periods. Hey, it could happen. I had just gotten into the best shape of my life. I thought I was building muscle when the scale started tipping upwards again... That was until my belly started to protrude.

I didn't know how I was going to do it. Have another child all by myself. I couldn't just tell Dustin he was a father now. For as much as I knew, he was still either in prison serving his time or perhaps in treatment in a facility. I had no way of contacting him, nor did I want to. The courts were so finicky, they could potentially order me to move back to allow him contact, and I couldn't do that. I couldn't uproot my children again. We were finally happy, and doing well. This child was definitely going to pose some issues, but I was determined to love it.

Now here I was...on a birthing table, half the world away from my parents and the baby's father, about to bring another child into the world.

"Okay, Naomi, you need to give a big push. You're almost there, you're crowning."

"Ok, ok, I can do it." I said it more to myself than to anyone else. There was no one there with me for support. I couldn't bring one of my kids. That would have been extremely inappropriate in my mind. I'd already had to break the news to them that they were going to have a new sibling. It hadn't gone over well.

"Three...two..PUSH!"

"Gahhhhhhh!!!" I hollered as I pushed with all my strength, my body quaking with pain and effort.

"OK, you're doing great! The head is out. One more big push and you're done!"

I sucked in, bared my teeth and heaved with all my might.

“There you go! Congratulations, Ms. Finstead, you’re a mommy again.”

The nurse handed me a small, naked babe, all purple and chalky. The umbilical cord was still attached, but I paid it no mind. I reached for my newest little one eagerly. The magic of birth, you forget the pain instantly, the worry, everything. All you care about anymore is that little one in your arms.

“It’s a boy.” I began to sob. He was so beautiful. His tiny little body so frail. He had a tuft of strawberry blonde hair that was darkened by the blood and mucus. His little hand reached up, and I held my finger up so he could grasp it. His tight little fist was barely able to stretch around my finger.

“I’m going to call you...Seth. Seth Joseph Trail.”

About Me

Creator and Author of the adult fiction Misguided Desires series. For those that don't already know me, I'd like to stay as inconspicuous as possible. The less you know about me, the more immersed in your reading experience you can get! I hope you all enjoy the books! If there's any feedback or requests for something you'd particularly love to read, I'd love to hear from you. Never hesitate to reach out. I always enjoy hearing from you and hearing your thoughts.

On a final note: Thank you all for your reading passion, it's the readers that make the author.

Keep watch for my new and exciting titles as they are released.

EMINENCE FRONT

The font used in this book is EB Garamond.
http://www.georgduffner.at/ebgaramond/index.html

Printed in the USA
CPSIA information can be obtained
at www.ICGtesting.com
JSHW080305220524
63234JS00001B/39

9 798223 528777